A Queer Kind of Death "was universally and deservedly praised by reviewers, but the inevitable sequel was even better. In SWING LOW, SWEET HARRIET, Baxt emerged as one of the finest of modern satirists."

— Jeff Banks
Twentieth Century Crime and Mystery Writers

By George Baxt:

*now available in a Crime Classic® edition.
**forthcoming from the IPL Library of Crime Classics®

GEORGE BAXT

SWING LOW, SWEET HARRIET

A CRIME CLASSIC ®

INTERNATIONAL POLYGONICS, LTD.
NEW YORK CITY

SWING LOW, SWEET HARRIET

Library of Congress Card Catalog No. 87-80310
ISBN 0-930330-56-0

Printed and manufactured in the United States of America
by Guinn Printing.
First IPL printing April 1987.
10   9   8   7   6   5   4   3   2   1

For my family (in order of appearance):
Samuel Baxt, Lena Baxt, Morris Baxt,
Juliette Terman, Estelle Brickel

1

IT WAS a rare day for August, with the temperature in the low seventies and the humidity in the low forties and the people crowding Broadway between West Seventy-second and West Seventy-third streets in uniformly high good humor. It was a day as rare as a Jewish teller at the Chase Manhattan Bank. The clock above the entrance to the bank at the corner of Broadway and Seventy-third indicated it was one minute before noon, and necks began to crane, ears began to strain toward the corner of Broadway and Seventy-second.

Another Wednesday, and Wednesday at noon had become a ritual for habitués of this particular area of New York's West Side. What occurred every Wednesday at noon (like clockwork) belonged to them and to them alone, and they treasured and hoarded the event with the same pride they treasured and hoarded Oscar's Noshery, the Tip-Toe Inn and the New Yorker movie house. There was nothing to equal them on the East Side (so West Siders claimed staunchly, fiercely, sometimes violently) and there was now positively nothing to equal what took place every Wednesday at noon, and had been taking place every Wednesday at noon for the past five months.

That February Wednesday, five months ago, when it first began, people were at first amazed, then embarrassed, and a member of the local B'nai B'rith chapter wanted to know why somebody didn't call the police. But it was over in three minutes, and the majority chose to pass it off as either a drunken indiscretion or a publicity stunt. Then it happened again the following Wednesday, and the Wednesday after that, and word began to spread and crowds began to gather and local merchants took advantage of the opportunity and advertised their most seductive bargains on Wednesdays.

The hands on the bank's clock became united as one, the noon sirens pierced the air, and a hush fell over Broadway between Seventy-second and Seventy-third. A baby started to whimper and the mother clamped her hand over its mouth, ignoring the purple tinge beginning to spread like a plague across the infant's startled face. A horse whinnied, and the mounted policeman jabbed his left spur into its flank and the animal seemed to gulp and hang its head in embarrassment. A Broadway bus ground to a halt and the passengers crowded against the windows, grimly reminding an elderly patriarch leaning on his cane of a train he had seen departing for Dachau.

> *"Tippy-tap-toe, tippy-tap-toe,*
> *My favorite da-a-a-ance.*
> *Tippy-tap-toe, tippy-tap-toe,*
> *Come on! Take a cha-a-a-ance!"*

All eyes were centered on the corner of Broadway and Seventy-second. The voice was high, piping and quavery, like voices heard on vintage phonograph records. But it was also clear and controlled, with professional self-assurance.

> *"Come on! Start swinging low!*
> *Come on! Start swinging high!*
> *Let me tippy-tap-toe you*
> *Right up to the sky!"*

"Vo-dee-oh-doe!" chanted the crowd in exuberant unison and right on cue as Sweet Harriet Dimple came singing and tap-dancing around the corner of Seventy-second Street, heading up Broadway to Seventy-third. She wore a white blouse with bolero sleeves and with "S.H.D." artistically embroidered over her left breast, a white accordion-pleated skirt that billowed out like an umbrella when she pirouetted (which was often), white gloves, white slippers tied by white laces, and a pretty white

bow in her hair, which was a tight cloche of blazing-red croquignoles.

> "*Tippy-tap-toe, tippy-tap-toe,*
> *My favorite da-a-a-ance.*
> *Tippy-tap-toe, tippy-tap-toe . . .*"

And then a series of precise, breathtaking high kicks to punctuate each syllable that followed.

> "*Will* . . . [kick]
>   *bring* . . . [kick]
>   *you* . . . [kick]
>   *to* . . . [kick]
>   *the* . . . [kick]
>   *land* . . . [kick]
>   *of* . . . [kick]
>   *ro* . . . [kick and pirouette]
>   *ma-a-ance!*"

With which she leaped inside the bank, the doors of which were held ajar for her by the two uniformed guards, who hadn't missed their cue in five months.

On Broadway, the mother removed her hand from the baby's mouth and the infant wept bitterly. The mounted policeman prodded his horse, which snorted somewhat contemptuously and broke into a slow walk. The bus driver revved his motor as the passengers returned to their seats and the crowd on the street slowly began to disperse. Some giggled, some shook their heads in wonder, and more than a few wiped a tear from misty eyes.

The shoeshine boy outside the Barricini Candy Shop patiently answered the questions being put to him by a chubby middle-aged lady clutching a chubby middle-aged Pekingese.

"Was that *her?*" she asked eagerly. "Was that *really* Sweet Harriet Dimple?"

"Lady," said the boy politely, "there can't be two of her."

"But I thought she was *dead!*"

He shook his head, grinning. "No, ma'am, that was Sweet Harriet Dimple in person. Alive—and, you saw for yourself, kicking."

"Seymour will never believe me," said the chubby middle-aged lady as she moved away, reminding herself there was still the shopping to be done for her husband's dinner.

The newspaper vendor at the corner of Broadway and Seventy-second Street took in professional stride the question-and-answer sessions that followed each Wednesday performance by Sweet Harriet Dimple.

"She ain't that old," he was telling three women, one of whom had ventured the guess that Sweet Harriet was at least sixty. "Looked her up in the *World Almanac*. She'll be fifty in October."

"Fifty!" snorted one of the women. "When I was just a kid she was already a star in pictures!"

"Started when she was fourteen," said the vendor authoritatively.

"Fourteen!"

"Fourteen," repeated the vendor, wondering if any of them would be good for a *Post* or a *World Journal*. "That's what she told Johnny Carson when he had her on the show last month. And nobody lies to Johnny Carson."

Inside the bank, Sweet Harriet Dimple stood on the short line at one of the tellers' windows, tapping her foot, humming "Tippy-Tap-Toe" and tightly clenching in her right hand a deposit slip and five crisp twenty-dollar bills. She nodded to people who managed to catch her eye and smile (a smile that was intended to signal, "You're one of us, girl" or "You're a real trouper, kid, and we're with you to the end"), but catching Sweet Harriet's eye was almost as impossible a feat as snapping a picture of the Loch Ness monster. Sweet Harriet always looked up. At ceilings, the sky, helicopters and birds. Looking up strengthened her chin muscles. It also helped avoid such annoying conversational byplays as "I remember you when I was a child" or "I saw you last night on the Late Late

Show in *Barclay Mill's Follies of 1930* and you were better than ever!"

Barclay Mill.

One might have detected a trace of a forlorn smile on Sweet Harriet's face. Dear Barclay. Dear dead Barclay. Dear dead murdered Barclay. Why do newspapers, magazines and assorted crime writers periodically attempt to renew public interest in your sordid, unsolved murder? Why, during the thirty-three years since you were buried (two mausoleums east of Mabel Normand, one north of Wallace Reid, two south of Alma Rubens and soon to be surrounded by Lilyan Tashman and Lew Cody), won't they let you lie in peace? Why did the press castigate me for throwing myself across your coffin, weeping bitterly, crying your name over and over again, overhearing Flora Fleur's venomous "Just like Pola Negri when they were burying Valentino"? Why won't they let you stay dead, Barclay? The secret is safe with me. No one will ever know, unless . . .

"Miss Dimple. You're holding up the line."

Sweet Harriet lowered her eyes from the ceiling and stared at the smiling face at the opposite side of the counter.

"Good afternoon, Mr. Grebbs," said Sweet Harriet in her little-girl squeak, a cross between Betty Boop and Baby LeRoy. "I was lost in thought."

"How'd it go today?" asked Mr. Grebbs, taking the deposit slip and the five crisp twenty-dollar bills.

"It went real zippety-do," beamed Sweet Harriet. "They came in right on cue, 'Vo-dee-oh-doe.'"

"Going to be on TV again?" asked Mr. Grebbs as he stamped the deposit slip and handed Sweet Harriet her receipt.

"The producer of *Girl Talk* is trying to arrange a date for me. I'll let you know if and when. 'Bye now."

Sweet Harriet folded the receipt neatly as she walked away from the counter, and placed it in the tiny white change purse she carried in one of the hidden pockets of her skirt.

"Miss Dimple?"

The voice startled her. She hadn't seen or felt anyone approach. People always caught her unaware when she thought about Barclay Mill.

"My name is Seth Piro."

Sweet Harriet lifted her head slowly and looked at what once must have been a handsome face. He was probably around forty, maybe more, maybe less, with deep black crevices under his eyes and tiny veins forming patterns on his cheeks and nose. But his warm smile displayed a set of beautiful white teeth, and how often had Sweet Harriet succumbed to warm smiles and beautiful white teeth.

"You haven't replied to my letters, or returned any of the messages I left at your hotel, so I decided to approach you in person."

Sweet Harriet's pout is familiar to all who have ever seen her on screen, and Seth recognized it now. "If I have chosen to ignore your entreaties, Mr. Piro," squeaked Sweet Harriet, "can't you take a hint?"

"If at first you don't succeed . . ." said Seth with a shrug. "Anyway, at least I got to hear you singing and watch you dancing in person. I'd been told it was a unique experience, but now that I've seen and heard for myself what can I say except . . . I have an exquisite new memory to treasure."

Sweet Harriet didn't move a muscle.

"Couldn't you possibly spare me half an hour?" The little-boy-lost look on his face was almost irresistible.

"You sure can pour on the booshwah," said Sweet Harriet, whose vocabulary was a repository for ancient, long-forgotten colloquialisms. "You must be Irish."

"No," smiled Seth, "I'm Greek."

"Greek," repeated Sweet Harriet, as her eyes fixed upon the ceiling again. "The only Greek I ever trusted was Spyros Skouras." For a few seconds there was silence as she became lost in thought again. Then: "There's a health-food store around the corner. Follow me there." She clickety-clacked past him, nodding to the two guards, who held the doors open for her, with Seth following.

The concoction Sweet Harriet was spooning into her mouth was called an Invigorator. It consisted of yogurt, blackstrap molasses and wheat germ. Seth toyed with a tall glass of blue-and-orange liquid that was listed in the menu as an Atlas Martini. He learned, too late, the mixture was a blend of pulverized carrots, tomatoes, asparagus and cabbage. Sweet Harriet had insisted on complete silence while she ate her Invigorator, and for ten minutes Seth watched the contents of her plate diminish. With the last spoonful demolished, Sweet Harriet dabbed at her mouth with a paper napkin and sat back in her chair, contemplating the ceiling.

"Does Madeleine Cartier know you've been trying to reach me?"

"Of course," said Seth. "It was she who suggested Wednesday."

Sweet Harriet abandoned the ceiling and fixed Seth with her iron-gray eyes.

"How long is it now," she asked coyly, "you've been collaborating on her autobiography?"

"Five months," replied Seth.

"What took you so long to get around to me?"

"Sixty-three reels of tape starring Madeleine Cartier."

"Sixty-three reels of tape," repeated Sweet Harriet slowly. "I bet they're a hoot."

"They're far from dull," said Seth, somewhat bemused. "In fact, in time they're likely to become collector's items."

"Like me. Like Madeleine. Like the Fleur sisters, and Bogie, and Bette, and Joan . . ." Her voice trailed away like a wisp of smoke as she stared at his untouched Atlas Martini.

"Don't you like it?" she asked, indicating the glass.

"It's not the kind of martini I prefer."

"I'll finish it, then," she said, reaching for the glass, "if you don't mind. Waste not, want not."

"Be my guest," said Seth.

Sweet Harriet's hand froze in mid-air.

"Is something wrong?"

"*He* used to say that all the time—" her voice quivered

as it was stirred by a breeze of memory—" 'Be my guest.' "

"Who do you mean?"

"Barclay Mill." She spoke the name softly, with reverence, and for a moment Seth thought he heard a fading echo of "Taps" being played on a trumpet. She sipped the drink, placed the glass on the table, and continued staring into it. "You know, of course, he discovered me."

"Yes."

"Thirty-six years ago." Seth had to strain to hear her. "I was thirteen at the time." She looked up. "Barclay Mill cornered the market on nymphets long before Vladimir Nabokov. I'll bet you never guessed I do a lot of reading. You have to turn to books when your friends run out on you, or you die of loneliness. I even have *you* in paperback."

"Which one?" asked Seth, intrigued. "I've written three."

"The one about the fag. *Ben, A Wasted Life.* You made it all up, didn't you?"

"No," said Seth, "it's all true."

"All of it?" she asked incredulously, looking for a moment like a child who couldn't believe she was being taken to the circus. "Really all of it? The way you felt about him? How you felt after he was found dead in his bathtub, electrocuted by a radio?" The beads of perspiration forming on Seth's brow did not escape Sweet Harriet.

"All of it."

"I don't believe you," she stated flatly.

"Let's talk about you and Madeleine." Seth reached into his pocket and brought out a miniature tape recorder. "You don't mind if I record our conversation, do you?"

"Collector's item?" Coy again, cocking her head coquettishly.

"It's more accurate than notes or my memory."

"If you're dying to light a cigarette, light one," she said suddenly. "Just don't blow the smoke in my face."

14

Seth didn't want a cigarette, but he lit one anyway, exhaling out of a corner of his mouth.

"It's suicide, you know," she said, after another sip of the "martini." "That's how they tried to pass off Barclay's murder. But I wouldn't let them. That finished me in Hollywood." The note of pride in her voice did not go undetected. "I never stopped loving Barclay even after he threw me over for Fauna Fleur."

Seth switched on the tape recorder.

"After Fauna Fleur," he prodded, "there was Madeleine, wasn't there?"

The iron-gray eyes pierced into his. "She didn't tell you that."

"No," admitted Seth, "but she said he made a play for her during the shooting of *Barclay Mill's Follies of 1932*. That was his last picture before he was murdered."

"He may have made a play for her, but they never had an affair." Her tongue was a gardener's shears clipping each word like an overgrown hedge. "They never found anything connecting her with Barclay, like they did me, and Flora and Fauna. We were the only three who really got clobbered. You know they're living over near Central Park."

"I have a date with them this afternoon. The Sisters Fleur. Flora and Fauna."

Sweet Harriet finally smiled, and it was a sweet smile. "They were the best acrobatic dancers in vaudeville, till Barclay signed them for the *Follies of '29*. The three of us made our picture debuts in that one. Madeleine didn't come along until 'thirty-two." Coy again. "I suppose you were too young to have seen us."

"I'm not too young for television. I've seen you."

"Well?"

"Enchanting."

"You're right," nodded Sweet Harriet, "we were absolutely enchanting." Her face hardened. "Not like those foreigners they're peddling today with their monstrous chests!" She made a tiny fist and slammed it on the table. "*We* didn't need breasts! We had *talent* then!" She jumped to her feet with a clickety-clack. "I have to go now."

Seth rose swiftly and barred her way. "But, Miss Dimple—I'm not finished!"

"*Don't* call me Miss Dimple," she snapped. "It sounds like one of those Shirley Temple pictures! Call me Sweet Harriet!" Then swiftly, "Tomorrow, three o'clock, my hotel." And she swept past him and out.

Oh God, oh God, he repeated to himself. Why did I let Ruthelma Kross sandbag me into ghosting these memoirs for Madeleine Cartier? Why'd I let myself be seduced with that advance from the publisher? Why didn't I just go away and drink myself into oblivion the way I had planned?

"A dollar fifty," he heard the waitress say.

"What?" She was standing next to him holding a green slip.

"A dollar fifty."

"Oh, yes," sighed Seth, fishing in his jacket pocket.

"She a friend of yours?" asked the waitress as Seth handed her two dollars.

"No," said Seth, pocketing the tape recorder. "Keep the change."

"She's a nut case," said the waitress, "and thanks."

"Sometimes I think we're all nut cases," said Seth, "and you're welcome."

Emerging from the store, Seth saw Sweet Harriet disappear around the corner. From a doorway near the corner, two tall young men, one blond, one dark-haired, stepped out and followed her. They were dressed in identical brown jackets and identical tan slacks, and kept in step until they disappeared around the corner.

"Tomorrow, three o'clock, my hotel."

Seth was beginning to get interested again.

2

———◄••►———

SWEET HARRIET studied the two handsome young men
from her vantage point in the outdoor phone booth. She
held the receiver to her ear and moved her lips occasionally to give the impression she was engaged in important
conversation. She hoped the two handsome young men
weren't as familiar with this phone booth as she was. On
three occasions it had swallowed and digested her dimes,
never rewarding her with a dial tone, the third bad ten-
cent investment finally convincing her the contraption
was out of order. But Sweet Harriet had long ago learned
how to turn adversity into an advantage. This booth was
now one of her several private sanctuaries, and her per-
formances at the long-ago-muted instrument were familiar and occasionally applauded by the local citizenry.

Once she had been seen shaking her tightly croquinoled
coiffure violently as she squeaked into the innocently
dumb mouthpiece, "Never, Darryl, never! I could never
take second billing to Julie Andrews!," her foot propping
open the folding door slightly so that the bravery would
penetrate eavesdropping ears for posterity. Only once
had a performance backfired, and that was the afternoon
she sternly advised David O. Selznick the role of Melanie
in a musical version of *Gone with The Wind* was not for
her, completely unaware the good gentleman had passed
away the previous evening.

Now her pantomime took a back seat to the concentration of her iron-gray eyes. Those iron-gray eyes never
missed a detail. The two handsome young men amiably
discussing the contents of a haberdashery display were
twins, though one was blond and the other dark-haired.
She considered the possibility that as children they might

have been labeled "His" and "Hers." Their brown jackets and tan slacks were superbly tailored, and Sweet Harriet's professional eye told her that beneath the apparel were muscular and well-proportioned bodies. Each sported a bachelor's-button in the lapel of his jacket, but the purple shirts and the orange-and-green striped ties were a dead giveaway.

They were from California.

Well, thought Sweet Harriet as she hung up the receiver, time to show those boys a bit of the old moxie. She pushed the booth door to one side with her left hand, cemented her right hand to her hip, narrowed her eyes into ominous slits, and slowly clickety-clacked toward the twins in her once-familiar toughly defiant gait that Clara Bow had tried to copy but could never master.

"Well, big boys," each word punctuated with a fearless toss of the croquignoles, "what's your racket?"

("No! No! No! No! *No!*" Barclay had cried in anguish after her fifteenth take. "The emphasis should be on 'Well,' not 'big boys'! You're showing them you mean business! For crying out loud, baby, what's wrong with you this morning? Fifteen takes! Jesus walked on water in one!")

The twins turned and stared at the five-foot bundle of simulated dynamite. The blond spoke first.

"I'm Peter."

Harriet thought her heart would stop. Hadn't she heard this soft, purring, mellifluous voice before?

The brunet smiled.

"I'm Robert."

Steady, girl, steady. That smile. That bone-melting smile. She tried to keep her voice from trembling when she spoke.

"You boys got nothing better to do than tail a star all morning? What are you selling? Subscriptions to the Literary Digest?"

"We've been waiting for an opportunity to speak to you," said Robert gently.

"We left a note at your hotel desk a few days ago,"

added Peter. "You seem to have chosen to ignore it, and that distressed us."

Sweet Harriet jogged her memory. Monday. "Dear Lady, May we request an audience on a matter of utmost importance. P. and R. Moulin."

"I get lots of notes left at the desk. It's always somebody wanting an autographed picture. Well, the clerk at the desk has stacks of them. Didn't he offer you a couple?"

Robert smiled. That smile. "We're after a different sort of souvenir."

"Sayyyyy," said Sweet Harriet, shifting from one foot to the other so that her right hip projected, emphasizing the elbow of the arm cemented to the hip, "what's the act?"

"We don't have an act," said Peter. "We simply wish to hold a conversation with you."

"No act, eh?" Sweet Harriet's upper lip curled as she spoke. (How many hours had Barclay kept her in front of the mirror until she perfected that look?) "Don't kid me, big boys. I wasn't born yesterday. You're twins. All twins have an act!"

"You *are* clever, Miss Dimple," purred Robert. "Don't you remember us from films, ohhh, some twenty years ago when we were mere tykes—the Moulin Twins? We were number three at the box office for two years, and then our beard stubble began to show."

"I thought there was something familiar about you two," admitted Sweet Harriet. "Well, what are you after now? A co-production deal in Italy or something?"

"Or something," nodded Peter. "We'd like to talk about Barclay Mill."

Sweet Harriet slowly lowered her right hand, which was beginning to get atrophied anyway, and stared at the handsome faces.

"Does it disturb you to talk about him?" Robert asked gently, studying Sweet Harriet's ashen face.

"No," squeaked Harriet, "not so much any more. Seems Barclay's due for a comeback without even trying. I just

19

shook another joker who's trying to pump me on him."

"Seth Piro," said Peter. "We know all about him. He's ghosting Madeleine Cartier's memoirs. He's written three books."

"The first two incredibly bad," interjected Robert.

"The more recent one," segued Peter, "a bit better, with a wealth of fascinating material about a case involving himself and a murdered ex-lover—with a solution Robert and I find most unsatisfactory."

"You see, Miss Dimple," added Robert (with that smile—where did he inherit that smile?), "we are now rather successful writers. We collaborate on books, specializing in unsolved crimes."

"So now you're trying to rake up poor old Barclay." A pert toss of the croquignoles that made Peter wonder what had become of Alice White.

"Actually," volunteered Peter, "we're compiling an anthology of unsolved Hollywood crimes. You know—the murders of Thelma Todd, William Desmond Taylor . . ."

"Barclay Mill." Those iron-gray eyes, thought Robert. What hidden secrets lay behind those iron-gray eyes?

Sweet Harriet thought a moment, eyes piercing the sky as though searching for some hidden god who might strike these twins with thunderbolts.

"Tomorrow . . . four o'clock . . . my hotel."

Like a tiny tornado, she spun on her heel and clickety-clacked toward Central Park. Peter looked at Robert, who was smiling at the tiny white clickety-clacking figure. He seemed to be reading Peter's mind as he said without looking at him, "No point in following her now. Tomorrow . . . four o'clock . . . her hotel. We can wait. We know how to wait. Let's have some lunch."

"Fauna."

"Not now, Flora!" There was a touch of irritation in the voice.

Fauna Fleur sat at a bridge table that held a portable radio. In the space between herself and the radio she carefully laid out a deck of cards. The syrupy-sweet strains of a popular orchestra drifted lazily from the radio as Fauna concentrated on each card she dealt as though it were a priceless jewel.

Flora Fleur remained standing in the doorway between the living room and the kitchen, filter-tip cigarette dangling precariously from her lower lip, drying a coffee pot with a dish towel. Amazing, Flora thought to herself, how Fauna's saucer-eyed, snub-nosed beauty seems to have remained undimmed these past thirty-odd years. There was still a fine line to her profile—unlike Flora's, which now supported two chins, two jowls, and a purplish puff under each eye. Dying her hair jet black had seemed only to emphasize the aging malformations of her visage, but what the hell, she'd never step before a movie camera again.

But Fauna was another story. What a testimony to the teachings of Yogi Absalom. Fauna had been a brilliant pupil. The yogi had given her inner peace, inner serenity, and seemingly eternal outer beauty. Thank God for the outer beauty. It helped keep her fairly busy in television commercials.

"Fauna, honey," a determined Flora said pointedly, "that Piro man will be here any minute now."

"Dammit, Flora!" screeched Fauna. "Didn't you hear me say 'Not now'?"

(Control yourself, thought Fauna, sure you have a headache. You're tense, irritable . . . Don't take it out on Flora—take an Anacin.)

"I'm sorry, dear," said Fauna, "I'll be finished with the cards in a few minutes, and I have a slight headache."

"Do you want an aspirin, honey?" Flora's concern was heartfelt. She knew Fauna's migraines as well as she knew her own bunions and the thirty-five-year-old calluses on her large, powerful hands.

Fauna had difficulty controlling the irritation in her voice when she replied to Flora's offer. "How many times have I told you, Flora, don't just say aspirin, say Anacin or Bufferin, something like that—never just Brand X."

It wouldn't have surprised Fauna if Flora's sigh was audible on the lower East Side, and that was a good three miles south of their small but comfortable fourth-floor walk-up apartment. Flora had gone through hell modulating her brass band of a voice when they were in talkies. (They'd always be "talkies" to Fauna.)

"You want an Anacin, then?" persisted Flora, face screwed up with agony as the smoke from her cigarette attacked her eyes, knowing she was momentarily defenseless holding pot and towel.

"*Please,* Flora."

Flora stormed into the kitchen, slammed the pot on the stove, jammed the dish towel on the rack, and drowned the cigarette stub in a downpour of tap water. Damn Fauna and damn her moods! Fifty years of goddamned Fauna moods! Petulant moods. Hunger moods. I-want-ice-cream moods. I-want-chow-mein moods. Frightening moods. Smiling moods. Horrifying moods. I'm-going-to-marry-Barclay-Mill-whether-you-like-it-or-not moods.

Would we still be stars today if it hadn't been for the damned scandal after Barclay's murder? Flora asked herself. She pondered the question at least once six days a week, twice on Sundays, and one for good measure when watching one of their old flicks on TV—Fauna usually weeping and sniffling into a Kleenex (from a pop-up box), Flora stony-eyed though aching inside from the piercing prongs of ancient, painful, undying memories.

Damn Madeleine. Damn damn Madeleine. (No, darling. I'm sorry. Forgive me. Not damn. Not really damn. You've always been good to us—Fauna and me. You have this chance to make a comeback and you have every right to try and make the most of it. Television series that are just right for you don't come along too often. A network and a sponsor willing to gamble on you, willing to gamble the public has forgiven you the scandals—and do you have to be scandal-prone?—you have every right to try and spring back from that hideous oblivion in which you've been sequestered these past five years. But the memoirs. Did you have to agree to the memoirs? A Pandora's box unleashing the furies with their fiercely evil, destructive force. Yes, you've still got some good years ahead of you, Madeleine darling. You have every right to make the most of this opportunity. Darling Bette made the most of hers. And Joan. And sweet Olivia. Sweet—Sweet Harriet. That frigging pain-in-the-ass soubrette! Following you to New York to try and hop on the bandwagon. Maybe she'll break both of those frigging tippy-tap-toe legs of hers.)

"You're talking to yourself again!" screamed Fauna.

"No I'm not!" Flora's reply tore through the apartment like a sonic boom.

"I can hear you muttering!"

"By Christ, if I want to mutter I'll mutter!"

"You're tense and nervous! Take a Compoz!"

"Screw Compoz! Screw everybody!"

The doorbell rang.

A sudden hush fell over the apartment like a velvet comforter. Flora removed her apron and flung it on a chair, and strode briskly into the living room. Unperturbed, Fauna was still hunched over the bridge table, studying the cards, deep in concentration.

The doorbell rang again. Hand on the knob, Flora turned to Fauna. "Remember—let me do the talking." Fauna pretended not to have heard her. Flora counted ten, which was all it usually took to calm herself down, and then, with her "We're auditioning for RKO-Keith-Proctor's time" smile, opened the door.

Seth stood in the doorway.

"Mr. Piro, I presume!" boomed Flora, hand briskly extended, with her hail-fellow-well-met standard greeting to strangers.

Seth shook her hand. "Flora or Fauna?"

"Flora! Come on in! That's Fauna! She'll be finished in a minute. She tells fortunes." Seth entered and Flora slammed the door shut, then indicated the sofa to Seth.

"He's got to stay out of that motorboat," whispered Fauna.

Flora met Seth's inquisitive look and smiled. "She's reading Guy Lombardo. How's about a drink?" She knew a hangover when she saw one.

"Well," smiled Seth, "I wouldn't mind a wee nip."

"Good man!" boomed Flora as she crossed to a sideboard groaning under the weight of two dozen assorted bottles of whiskies, wines and liqueurs. Wee nip, she thought. The kid's got a bad case of Barry Fitzgerald. Wee nip. She could match that.

"Name your poison!"

"Scotch," requested Seth.

"Which brand?" interjected Fauna without looking up from the cards.

Flora knew how to deal with a startled look. "Fauna does commercials. She dotes on brand names."

"Of course," said Seth, trying to remember if this morning's horoscope in the *Daily News* had warned him there'd be Sweet Harriet Dimple followed by Fauna and Flora Fleur and at least another nine hours of this day left to cope with. "Do you have Vat Sixty-nine?"

"I should have guessed," ventured Flora sweetly as she selected the bottle and poured a stiff shot into a glass. "Water or soda?"

"Just some ice." He realized Fauna was now staring at him. He turned to her and smiled. "Hello. I'm Seth Piro."

"A good name," nodded Fauna. "It would look well on a marquee." She arose from her chair, crossed to the couch and sat next to Seth, taking his right hand and staring down at his palm.

"Hmmm." She was deep in thought. Flora winked at Seth as she handed him his drink.

"Hmmmm," Fauna hmmm'd again, as Flora settled into an easy chair and lit a cigarette, her too tight skirt hitching up as she crossed her muscular legs, revealing rolled stockings and one inch too many of blue-veined thighs.

"Fascinating," said Fauna, closing Seth's hand, then rising and returning to the bridge table.

"Is that all?" asked Seth, somewhat startled.

"Give her time to gestate," said Flora warmly. Then to Fauna, "Are you finished with the cards, dear?"

"Yes, dear." Fauna was stacking the deck neatly.

Flora studied Seth and exhaled in rapid succession three halos of smoke rings. "Madeleine told us to be terribly cooperative. How's it going?"

"Madeleine's an ever-gushing fountain of memories," Seth replied, then treated himself to his first sip of the Scotch. "I've got sixty-three tapes of her reminiscences."

"Sixty-three!" gasped Flora. "That ought to be enough for a couple of volumes!" "Volume" was a word that came easily to Flora, and Seth wondered if it was her voice or a passing truck that caused the walls to tremble.

"About half of it is usable," Seth confided. "Which brings me to what I call the *Citizen Kane* period of my research. You know—what her friends, co-workers, et cetera, can tell me about her. Some anecdotes, some jokes . . ."

"Jokes!" erupted Flora. "Did you hear the one about the farmer's daughter with the cleft palate—"

"Jokes about Madeleine," interrupted Seth gently. "Madeleine came to Hollywood in 1932. Wasn't that when you first worked together?"

Flora lifted her left hand and surveyed the fingernails for a few moments. "She was the prettiest kid you ever saw. Big blue eyes, lovely blond hair—natural, too— great figure. Sang and danced up a storm. And a great sense of humor she knew how to display to advantage. You know—sort of like Carole Lombard. Barclay Mill knew how to pick a winner."

"Was Mill ever in love with her?"

"Love?" It was Fauna who spoke. She sat with her hands folded in her lap, and Seth had to strain to hear her. " 'Love' didn't define too easily for Barclay. 'Affection' is a better word, though still not quite accurate. Girls held a place in Barclay's affections. Tenures never lasted longer than a few months or so. I was his last. There was no time to replace me. He was murdered before he could make a choice. I suppose that's why I'm less bitter then the others. Though I don't think he made as big a fuss over me as he did when he was having Sweet Harriet Dimple."

"Having" grated on Seth's ears.

"She made a terrible fuss at his funeral."

"Fuss!" snorted Flora. "When she threw herself across that coffin, I expected the damn thing to collapse and Barclay to rise up screaming 'Cut!' Have you met our sweet Sweet Harriet?"

"A few hours ago."

"Did you get to catch the 'Tippy-Tap-Toe' routine first?"

"I sure did," sighed Seth. "It was quite a show."

"She was always an exhibitionist," grumbled Flora. "You know how she got started in squawkies? Hung by her teeth from a rope suspended from a Goodyear zeppelin circling Hollywood!" Roaring with laughter, she slapped her knee with her hand, joggling ashes from her cigarette onto the rug. "You have to hand it to the bitch! You may as well, she'll take it anyway! What an operator. Trailed Madeleine here from the Coast to see if she can squeeze her way into that TV series Madeleine's going to do."

"She won't," whispered Fauna. She met Seth's inquisitive look. "I read her cards last week. It's not in the cards for Sweet Harriet."

Flora cocked her head jovially toward Fauna. "How do you like the Sorcerer's Apprentice? Reads cards, tea leaves and, when she's really inspired, coffee grinds. That's how we lived after Barclay's murder rocked Hollywood and we were out, o-u-t. Came back East and Fauna got a job in a gypsy tearoom run by a Mrs. Horowitz, a Rumanian gypsy. *I* demonstrated cosmetics at Woolworth's. Guess you can't tell now I once had quite a face."

Seth was about to say, "It's still quite a face," but caught himself. Instead, "Didn't your studio try to rescue your careers? After all, they had a lot of money invested in you, Fauna and Sweet Harriet."

"Peanuts compared to what they would have lost if they had tried to clear us. All them do-goody religious organizations threatened a boycott unless we were bounced. So we were bounced. All because them letters all of us wrote Barclay were found by some reporter and spread across every front page in the country. Poor

Fauna. Just when she was about to be loaned out for the biggest role of her career. But that went to—"

"Don't mention her name!" It was the loudest Fauna had been since Seth's arrival. "Just don't *ever* mention her name!" Her voice broke, and she fled to what Seth assumed was a bedroom.

Flora uncrossed her legs, looked at the door behind which Fauna had hidden herself, then leaned forward conspiratorially to Seth. "She lost the job to—" She flung another furtive look toward the door, then whispered, "Ruby Keeler."

"Rub—!"

"Sssssh!" hissed Flora. "She'll hear you. Ruby's an adorable kid and all that, but Fauna will never get over losing that part. Imagine! Thirty-three years later she still bears a grudge. Now. Back to Madeleine. After Barclay signed her for *Follies of '32* he was preparing to star her in *Follies of '33,* when whoever bumped him bumped him. While the studio was trying to decide whether or not to drop Madeleine's option along with the rest of us—not that they had anything on *her,* but you know, guilt by association and all that—she became such a mental wreck worrying, she had that nervous breakdown. So Fauna and I took her to Mexico. Six months later she was headed back to Hollywood for a fresh start, which, as the world knows, she got, and Fauna and I took a bus to New York and oblivion."

Flora paused and listened.

"Something wrong?" asked Seth.

"I hear something. You don't happen to be bugged, do you?"

Seth removed the miniature tape recorder from his jacket pocket and held it up. "Forgive me. I have a rotten memory. It seemed to make Sweet Harriet nervous when I tried to interview her earlier, so I decided to keep it hidden when I came here. Do you mind?"

"Hell, no! Looks nice! Leave it out! Now, where was I?"

"You were on a bus to oblivion."

She guffawed. "Yeah! But Madeleine was okay. She told you, I suppose, she met Sam Wyndham, the camera-

27

man, down in Cuernavaca, where he was working on this here movie about the Mexican Revolution, and married him."

"Yes, and he was instrumental in helping revive her career."

"He was instrumental all right," roared Flora. "Always out tooting. Still, she stuck by him for ten years, which ain't bad for Hollywood—though he was in Spain for a couple of years shooting the war and then went off to the Pacific for the government. Seen Sam yet?"

"Tonight. He's invited me to his Film Society screening of the *Follies of '32*."

"Oh, well, that's great! We'll see you there! Poor Sam." She shook her head sadly. "He's sure fallen on sad times. But what the hell, he's got a great collection of old movies and has a ball running this Film Society of his. Madeleine says he's going to have a lot of that East Side camp crowd there tonight. Seems Barclay Mill pictures are 'in' these days again. You know the bunch I mean. That Baby Lake Sturgeon and her bunch. Ever been to one of his screenings before?"

"No. Tonight's my debut."

"Prepare yourself! Gets a crowd of creeps the likes of which you haven't seen since those old Karloff and Lugosi horrors. Movie buffs! They sit around all night arguing the name of the picture in which Fifi D'Orsay first picked her nose. Oh, what the hell. Why kick? They keep our memory alive!"

Fauna emerged from the bedroom with a wisp of a smile on her face.

"Forgive me, Mr. Piro. I've had a trying morning. I shot a commercial on location in a laundromat. It's one of a series I do. Perhaps you've seen me. I'm Mrs. Filth. I make everyone's laundry whiter and brighter without using ammonia. Anyway, we had to put the laundry through the washer four times and use a little ammonia before it was anywhere near the white they needed. And I'm just a bit exhausted."

"That's all right," smiled Seth. "I understand." He indicated the tape recorder. "What I've got now is fine for starters. Can we have another session later this week?" He and Flora rose simultaneously.

"Sure we can!" she boomed. "When we see you tonight at Sam's, we'll 'make date,' as they scribble on all the best men's rooms' walls!" She clapped Seth on the back and it took an effort to keep him from sagging at the knees.

Seth remembered something as Flora walked him to the door. "By the way, when Sweet Harriet left me this afternoon I think she was being followed by two men." Slowly Fauna sank onto the bridge chair as Flora's face seemed to drain of blood. "I only saw them from the back, but they were dressed as though they might have been twins."

"Well!" Flora finally managed to say. "We'll have to ask her about that! She'll probably be at Sam's tonight." Flora wrenched the door open. "See you later, now!"

Seth turned to Fauna, who sat rigid, staring at the floor. "We never did get back to my palm, did we?"

Fauna looked up slowly. "What? Oh! No—" very quietly—"no, we didn't. I'm sorry. I just wasn't up to it. Goodbye."

"Goodbye."

Seth stepped into the hall, and the door shut behind him.

Because I have sinned, dear God, he said to himself, must I pay for it the remainder of my life? Then he remembered he hadn't finished the Scotch, cursed under his breath, and headed for the staircase.

In the Fleur apartment, Flora crossed to Fauna and chucked her gently under the chin. "Cheer up, baby. I'll make us a cup of tea."

"Those two men," said Fauna, "those two men following Sweet Harriet . . ."

"Probably Peter and Robert. Madeleine warned us they were in town. I can handle them. Don't you worry your pretty head about it. I think you disappointed that Piro creep by not telling him what you saw in his palm."

"I couldn't," whispered Fauna, "I couldn't. What I saw was too terrible. Too, too terrible . . ."

3

His MESSAGE SERVICE informed Seth that Mr. Love would be free to join him that night and that Madeleine Cartier needed to see him urgently. Mr. Love *would* be free tonight of all nights, when it was imperative he attend the screening at Sam Wyndham's Film Society. What would Madeleine, Wyndham, the Fleur Sisters and iron-gray-eyed Sweet Harriet think he was up to when he introduced the Negro detective? After the first wave of the shock passed when they learned (if necessary) that he shared an apartment with Pharoah Love? (Why "shock"? Aren't thousands of men sharing apartments in New York?) What would the reactions be when they learned he was a detective? They were all once involved in a murder case that was still unsolved, and Seth had been questioning them about the victim. Would they think there was more to it than just seeking research for Madeleine's autobiography?

Why should I give a damn what they think? thought Seth.

Because I know how they feel.

Its all there in my book *Ben, A Wasted Life* (one printing in hard cover, after a polite reception from the critics, and doing better in paperback, thanks to an extremely lurid cover).

Will Ben's case one day be revived and raked over by an astute crime writer as Barclay Mill's is frequently revived and raked over? Will a crime writer one day come up with the real solution to Ben's murder? I live in fear of that.

Will a crime writer one day come up with the real solution to Barclay Mill's murder?

They live in fear of that—because I know how they feel.

I have seen their fear when I mentioned the murdered film director's name. But I am not here to threaten you or frighten you, my friends. I am here to do research into the life of the one, the only, the never-to-be-forgotten and God knows needs-no-introduction Madeleine Cartier.

"Hello! Hello-o-o! Hello-o-o-o-o-o! You darling man! You got my message and hurried right over!"

Seth hadn't realized he had walked to Madeleine's hotel on Central Park West, entered the elevator, emerged on the fifteenth floor, and rung the bell of her comfortable three-room suite. She stood in the doorway smiling brightly, wearing a filmy negligee bedecked with ostrich feathers, holding a glass of champagne in her left hand. There was a cacophony of noise from the living room, provided by three television sets going full blast.

"What's going on?" shouted Seth as he entered.

"A Madeleine Cartier festival!" she cried gleefully, shutting the door.

On the twenty-five-inch-screen color console, Madeleine was galloping to General Custer's rescue. On the twenty-one-inch black-and-white portable, Madeleine was releasing bombs over Tokyo, shouting, "And *that's* for Pearl Harbor!" And on the tiny six-inch Sony, Madeleine stood at a scaffold gravely intoning, " 'Tis a far, far better thing I do now than I have ever done before . . ."

Madeleine studied the Sony gravely. "I told them changing Sidney Carton to a woman would never work, but then"—gaily waving her hand—"there seemed to be no other point in remaking *A Tale of Two Cities!*"

With a rueful shake of her head, she walked from set to set, switching them off. As Seth watched Madeleine, he was reminded of the legend superimposed on various films he had seen: "Somewhere in France." The legend superimposed over Madeleine was "Somewhere in Her Forties." Forty-eight, probably, if his research was accurate. She looked ten years younger.

Madeleine caught him staring at her. "A penny for them," she said.

"Not worth the price," Seth replied amiably, and sank into an easy chair as Madeleine crossed to the champagne cooler and lifted the bottle.

"A sip of old tiddly? It's domestic wearing false colors, but not too bad if you have an active imagination."

"No, thanks. Any Scotch?"

"Of course, darling. Neat with a bit of ice, right?"

"Right."

In a few moments Seth had his Scotch and Madeleine was curled up on the couch opposite him. She began rubbing her forehead, and Seth had come to recognize what the gesture augured. Madeleine was troubled.

"Now, Seth," she began.

"Yes?"

"Well, it's like this." She rearranged herself on the couch. "It's all this delving into the Barclay Mill period of my life."

Seth leaned forward. "It's a very important period in your life. It's your start in Hollywood and—"

"I know, I know, I know," she interrupted, "but it's worrying the girls."

Seth didn't have to ask if she meant Sweet Harriet and the Fleur sisters.

"I only asked some routine questions. In fact, I didn't get much of anything from any of the three ladies. They were all a bit reticent."

"Well, you have to understand, darling," said Madeleine with what she hoped was a tone of affection, "the damn mess did ruin their lives. So you can understand they find rehashing it somewhat painful."

"Madeleine, may I remind you that when I accepted the offer to ghost this book you agreed it would be an honest and candid document, right?"

"Right. But . . ."

"But what?"

"Well, there's honest and there's honest, and there's candid and there's candid, isn't there?"

Seth got to his feet and began pacing the room as he

spoke. "The publishers *warned* you they didn't want an expanded fan-magazine puff! And I told you I wouldn't write that kind of tripe! I've got sixty-three tapes of your reminiscences, and you know what most of it adds up to? Your credits, how the critics rated them, who came to your parties, who didn't come to your parties, and how you learned to keep house after the film and TV offers dropped off five years ago."

"But I told you how Barclay once made a pass at me! Isn't that enough?"

"No that's *not* enough! His unsolved murder is still a ticket seller when the crime mags and the Sunday supplements rerun the story. *You* can't just pass it off with a few sentences. The Fleur sisters and Sweet Harriet Dimple are your oldest friends. You were all together on his last picture. Then he was murdered. There was a scandal. Three careers were ruined and yours was almost nipped in the bud."

"I'm always being nipped in the bud, dear," she sighed. "But that's neither here nor there. Look at it this way—and for God's sake sit down—" He sat. "I've got an important TV series coming up. Well, then. Supposing the series is going great guns and then my autobiography is published, including all the sordid details of the Barclay Mill case. Can you imagine how many of my self-righteous viewers will *not* be buying the product I'm peddling?"

"Not in this day and age, Madeleine. Don't try to hand me that. Mr. and Mrs. America dote on sordid details these days. It's the age of enlightenment. Look at all the publicity this series has been getting you. Has anyone tried to strong-arm the network or the sponsor into canceling the whole idea?"

"Dear God, I hope not!"

"You're perfectly safe, lovey, because they want *you* and *you alone!* New generations have rediscovered Madeleine Cartier, thanks to your old films on the tube. So you figured in a couple of scandals. Better yet. It adds spice to the new image. And the book will add spice to the spice. What are these broads afraid of? The murder happened thirty-three years ago. For all we know the killer is safe in his grave or—" He stopped.

Madeleine was stirring up the bubbles in her champagne with her index finger. "Or what?" she asked quietly.

"Or still alive."

Because I know how they feel.

"Can I have another Scotch?"

"Help yourself."

He crossed to the liquor cabinet and refilled his glass, then stood there staring at Madeleine.

"You know," she said with a sudden lilt to her voice, "my beloved ex-husband Mr. Wyndham had, and for all I know still has, a favorite and very pertinent expression, to wit, 'Every man for himself.' It's about time I started practicing what he preached. I told the girls to cooperate with you and they will. Face it. What they don't tell you about Barclay's murder you can always look up yourself. What the hell!" She arose and slammed the champagne glass down on an end table and lit a cigarette. "This is Cartier's last stand. I'm not kidding myself. I may as well make the most of it. If the series goes, I'm back on top again. If it flops, I've had it forever. I've got my annuities to keep me warm, though God knows there's a big enough drain on them." She stopped, inhaled, and then turned to Seth. "Why not? Let's give the damn book all I've got. Let the lawyers worry about what to omit. Damn it all! If I hadn't been such a fool five years ago, there'd be none of this to cope with."

She was now standing at a window staring out at Central Park. "Dear, darling Sam." The voice was grim and ominous. "I was always a soft touch for Sam. It was because of Sam I got involved with Rocco Mozzarella. Sam owed him a fortune in gambling debts and Rocco was putting the heat on him. So like a damn fool I go to see Rocco and beg him to give Sam a break—" turning away from the window and slowly crossing the room to the champagne cooler—"either that or lay out the cash myself. And I've done enough laying out for Sam."

En route to the cooler she retrieved her glass. "I suppose it was inevitable *Mister* Mozzarella and I get the hots for each other. You know how stormy and tempestuous that little romance was." She refilled her glass. "But did the son of a bitch have to start beating me up in my kitchen and trip and fall on that bread knife I happened to be holding?"

"Fate," commented Seth wryly, "can play some cruel tricks."

"It cost me a fortune to beat that rap," she sighed, "and it cost me my career in pictures." She plopped onto the couch, patting the space next to her. "Come sit here, sweetheart."

Seth obeyed.

"Would you like to escort me to that Film Society showing tonight?"

Mr. Love *would* be free tonight of all nights.

"I'd love to, but would you mind if the guy I share my apartment with joins us? I promised to take him."

A quizzical expression blossomed on Madeleine's face. "Funny. We've been working together for five months, and I never knew you lived with anyone. In fact, all I do know is what I read in that book of yours. I guess that's why I like you. In a way, we're sisters under the skin—if you'll pardon the expression." Gently she began to rub his cheek. "What's become of that wife of yours?"

"Ex-wife, thank you very much." Now her finger tips were tracing tiny circles on his cheek. "She's living in Mexico City with Daniel Saber, the man who published my first two books. It was a hard fight, Mom, but she separated him from the wife and kiddies and may God have mercy on both their souls."

"No lady in your life since?"

"Ohhh, there's been Sweet Harriet Dimple, and Fauna Fleur, and Flora Fleur—" he turned to her, smiling— "and Madeleine Cartier."

She leaned forward and kissed him. It was short, it was gentle, it was delicate and laudably professional. Other than the impact of her lips, Seth felt nothing.

Madeleine smiled as she patted his cheek. "Don't let it bother you. I'm a great one for collecting samples. Now tell me—what did you think of Flora and Fauna?"

"Fauna started to read my palm, but never told me what she saw."

"Probably indulging in one of her many moods," commented Madeleine darkly. "How dare she leave your palm unread? And how did Sweet Harriet strike you?"

Seth moved to the chair opposite the couch, Madeleine watching him with a sly and knowing smile. I made a pass and it made him uncomfortable, she thought to herself. I must be losing my grip, or I tried to grip at something that doesn't exist. She wiped the smile from her face when she realized Seth was talking.

"Sweet Harriet," he said, leaning back and crossing his legs, "didn't quite tippy-tap-toe her way into my heart. Our conversation was brief and cryptic. In fact, after five minutes I felt myself drowning in a sea of enigma. She did insist you never had an affair with Barclay Mill."

"I never said I did."

"Check. And if your comeback succeeds, I get the impression she plans to ride in on your coattails."

"Yes, she's looking forward to that trip." Madeleine was running her finger nervously around the lip of the champagne glass. "There's not a hope in hell for her, you know."

"Does Sweet Harriet know?"

"If she did, I'd have felt the repercussions by now."

"How does she live?"

"On dreams."

"I mean where does she get her money?"

"From faithful friends."

"Why didn't Sweet Harriet go with you and the Fleur sisters to Mexico after Mill's murder?"

"She stayed behind to put up a fight for her career. Pour me some more tiddly, will you, dear?" As Seth obliged, Madeleine began plinking the side of the glass with her thumb and index finger. (Nerves, thought Seth, a bundle of very exposed nerves.) "Sweet Harriet," continued Madeleine, "is quite a fighter. You have to admire her for that. Only she would dare that outrageous Wednesday exhibition of hers. Outrageous exhibitions are her backbone. But she always came running when I was in trouble, even unasked. Like that time during the war the U.S.O. shipped me back from Africa. All because of that incident in the bush with that Senegalese warrior."

Seth almost dropped the bottle as he refilled her glass.

"There was no convincing them *his* morale had also been a bit shaky," she began raging, "but of course there was that bit with the spear. . . . Oh, the hell with it. Flora's right. I'm scandal-prone. Dear God! Get me through this series without headlines!"

"Madeleine," said Seth, back in his seat, clasping his glass of Scotch with both hands, "I want to retrace everything we've discussed the past five months."

"Why, for crying out loud?"

"Because I've already found an important discrepancy. Flora said you met Sam Wyndham in Cuernavaca, where you married him. But you must have known him before then. He was Barclay Mill's favorite cameraman."

"Of course I knew him before then! What Flora meant was we ran into Sam *again* in Cuernavaca, and that was where the romance blossomed. He'd always had his eye on me, I later learned, and I was extremely vulnerable at the time, so when he proposed I married him. You mustn't take people so literally."

"I have to check and recheck the facts. That's my job."

"All right! All right! All right!" It was impossible to ignore the edge in her voice. "We'll go over all sixty-three tapes and I'll pay for my sins of omission!" The champagne glass was slammed down on the table again, and Seth marveled that it didn't shatter. It was as unbreakable as Madeleine and friends. Did a rare texture exist in the era in which these women were created, the secret of which has since disappeared?

"Something else," Seth resumed. "Two men followed Sweet Harriet when she left me earlier today." Madeleine's face remained strangely placid. "They were dressed alike, marched in step, and though I didn't get a look at their faces I got the impression they might have been twins."

"Really? I must ask Harriet about that when I see her later. She'll be delighted to hear that the outdoor concert in Central Park tomorrow night will be featuring medleys from Barclay Mill films—weather permitting. I've promised to put in an appearance." She was on her feet again, drawing the ostrich negligee tighter around her. "I might even treat them to one or two hits of my own."

"*San Di-e-go!*" she began belting in her powerful contralto. "*There's where they dock them ships. . .*" her hands forming tiny fists and sparring in space, "*that's where my ruby lips . . .*" gently wiggling her behind, "*plan to meet yours!*" She sank back onto the couch. "They don't write them like that any more. Can you and your friend pick me up around seven? I feel like a nap now."

"Seven on the dot." Seth crossed to Madeleine and put his hand under her chin. "Don't start getting depressed. You've got everything going for you."

"Sure," she murmured, "sure."

She continued to stare disconsolately at the floor, oblivious to Seth's exit. Then with a sob she rushed to the phone, picked up the receiver and began jiggling the hook frantically. "Plug it in, you goddamned extra! Plug it— Hello? Operator! Get me the Bramford Hotel. I want to talk to Harriet Dimple. *Sweet Sweet Sweet Sweet* Harriet Dimple!"

4

"HI THERE, cat! You look bushed."

"You get bushed beating around them." Seth slammed the door and crossed toward the bedroom, loosening his tie and removing his jacket.

"Get my message?" Pharoah Love sat in an easy chair, stripped to his shorts and nursing a very dry vodka martini on the rocks.

"I always get your message." Seth's words zeroed in from the bedroom and tickled Pharoah's stomach. He chuckled at the sensation. He accepted Seth's frequent testiness as he accepted the frequent tedium of police investigations. You can accept any adversity when you've got what you want.

"Bad day, cat?" he called out.

"Pour me a Scotch."

"I'm weary, cat. Pour your own." His well-proportioned coffee-skinned body settled deeper into the chair, legs outstretched and crossed at the ankles.

Seth entered, stripped to shorts and shirt, face darkened with irritation, and poured himself a Scotch.

"Madeleine cat getting you down, baby?"

"Madeleine cat big fat pain in my ass. And don't you start nibbling where she left off. Did you get that stuff from California yet?"

"Right there on your desk, cat. In the brown manila envelope."

Seth crossed to the desk and opened the envelope. It contained a thick file of Xeroxed papers, the top sheet headed "Barclay Mill. Confidential." "Read any of it?" asked Seth.

"Some. It has to be back in L.A. in a week. Them California cats don't like us New York cats poaching on their territory. Mr. Mill is still a big thorn in their sides. Seems a pair of twin cats got permission to go through the stuff a few weeks ago." Seth turned and stared at Pharoah. "Then came our request for the stuff. Coincidences make them nervous."

Seth was now sitting opposite Pharoah. "I saw a set of twins today tailing Sweet Harriet Dimple."

"Uh huh," smiled Pharoah lazily, "Peter and Robert Moulin. Six foot two. Brown jackets. Tan slacks. Purple shirts. Orange-and-green striped ties. Very pleasant and smile a lot."

"Sweet Harriet report them?" asked Seth.

"No, cat," drawled Pharoah, his matter-of-fact tone proving more of an abrasive on Seth's ears then the detective realized. "They favored the precinct with a personal appearance a few hours ago."

"Well, come on!" Seth erupted. "What did they want?"

Pharoah wagged an index finger. "Patience, patience. They are writers. They collaborate on true crime stories. They asked to see the file on Ben Bentley. Your hand's shaking, cat. You'll spill your drink."

"Did they see the file?" Seth's voice was an hysterical falsetto.

"Calm yourself, baby cat, calm yourself. Sure I let them see it. They had a letter of introduction from my buddy on the L.A. force. He got me the Mill file, didn't he? Gotta reciprocate in this business or people get a mad on—or even suspicious."

"Are you sure they weren't cops? Private investigators?"

"You're singing in high C, cat. Take a swig of that Scotch, count ten, and then listen." Seth swigged, counted ten, and listened, though the knuckles of his hand holding the glass were white and straining against the skin.

"You got nothing to worry about. You've seen the file often enough. You know it by heart. It adds up to Adam Littlestorm murdered Ben Bentley, and the mathematician doesn't live who can come up with a different total. I warned you something like this would pop up sooner or later. Ben cat's case made headlines, what with screwy Jameson-Ella cat puncturing Indian cat at that party. The twins won't be the first. A year from now, two, maybe three, someone else will decide to do a rehash. Most of it's in your book, anyway."

"Why'd they follow Sweet Harriet? Why not me?"

"I don't know, cat. I do not read minds. I only plumb them. Maybe they didn't know who you were." He shrugged. "Figure it for yourself. They went through the Barclay Mill file a few weeks ago. Probably doing a story on it. They come to New York and kill two birds with one. Ben cat's story and the Mill cat's story. The cast of characters is right here. Don't let it bother you."

"It bothered the Fleur sisters when I mentioned it to them."

"You've really had a busy day, haven't you? Sweet Harriet, the Fleur sisters, Madeleine cat."

"But Madeleine didn't bat an eyelash when I told her."

"That's because our Madeleine is the coolest cat of all. I'd like to meet that chick one of these days. I used to dig her a lot."

"Take a bath. You're meeting her tonight. We're escorting her to a screening of *Barclay Mill's Follies of 1932* at Sam Wyndham's Film Society."

"I do declare, Miss Scarlett"—a bad imitation of Butterfly McQueen—"I shall have to dress my prettiest."

"And try to play it cool." Seth's tone of voice demanded close attention. "She only found out today we keep house together."

"Uh huh."

Seth couldn't resist. "She also made a play for me."

"Miss Cartier," murmured Pharoah on his way to the bathroom, "Pharoah cat just might scratch your pretty eyes out."

Seth heard the torrent unleashed into the bathtub by Pharoah, and tried to dam the torrent of fear unleashed in his heart. That organ was thumping away like a jungle drum warning neighboring tribes of imminent danger. And thoughts of imminent danger crowded Seth's head like a subway crush. Peter and Robert Moulin. The names were familiar. Had he read something they had written?

Louis Armstrong's voice came growling from the radio in the bathroom. Hello, Dolly. Good night, Chet. Good night, David.

"Hey, cat! Come in here and talk to me! I'm lonesome."

Sweet Harriet slammed down the receiver and burst into tears. Two hundred photographs of her that would have made the creator of the before-and-after ads envious stared at her sob-racked body with pity. Blue mascara streams coursed down her cheeks, forming miniscule puddles in the creases of the fingers clamped to her mouth. Suddenly the fingers parted and Sweet Harriet shrieked, "Barclay, Barclay, Barclay!" Hearing his name soothed her. Her head fell listlessly against the back of the rocking chair, and she stared out the window at the row of television antennas on the roof of the building across the street. Then she whispered to herself, "I am dying, Egypt."

Like hell I am! She was beating the arms of the rocker with her bony little fists. Not this spunky kid! Nobody gives Sweet Harriet Dimple the old twenty-three skiddoo! Thanks for the buggy ride, eh, Madeleine? That's what you think, kiddo. What I knew thirty-three years ago is still good today, and you damn well know it.

"Damn well know what, dear?" said the Bronx-accented voice from the receiver. Sweet Harriet hadn't realized she had picked up the phone.

"I was talking to myself, Elsie," she squeaked. She gave Elsie a number and waited patiently.

"Hello!" boomed the voice at the other end.

"Now, you listen to me and you listen carefully," squeaked Sweet Harriet, "or the walls come tumbling down! Get me, big girl?"

In a building on East Fifty-sixth Street that specialized in renting meeting rooms and halls, Sam Wyndham stood in the doorway of the small auditorium on the ground floor collecting dollar bills from members of his Film Society and their guests. He prayed the air conditioner wouldn't break down, as it usually did. His clientele were riper than usual in August. He nodded jovially to familiar faces who greeted him, wondering where they hid themselves the other six days of the week.

"Sam!" screeched a bent, wizened old man in his seventies, waving an eight-by-ten glossy photograph in Sam's face. "Found a new photo of Aileen Pringle! That makes two thousand eight hundred and seventy-three in my collection." And thereby, thought Sam, setting a new world's record.

"Are they really coming?" gushed a peroxide-blond young man in his twenties, known affectionately to his friends as Lad, A Dog.

"They promised they'd be here, Marty," replied Sam to Lad, A Dog. "I'm positive Sweet Harriet and the Fleur sisters will show up."

"But Madeleine's *got* to come! I promised Mommy I'd bring her her autograph." Mommy was Lad, A Dog's uncle, also a movie buff but bedridden since struck by a car and paralyzed from the hips down when he chased Rock Hudson across Fifth Avenue for an autograph.

Madeleine, thought Sam, as he collected another dollar bill. How did I ever let her slip through my fingers? I should have known scandal can never stop her, the way rain, sleet and hail can't stop our trusted carriers from their appointed rounds. The hell with it. I've still got a hold on her. I'll never join the One Hundred Neediest Cases as long as Madeleine still breathes.

"Good evening, Samuel," said the *grande dame* in the doorway, sporting a Queen Mary hat undoubtedly once worn by Queen Mary, body encased in the red velvet cape she wore twelve months of the year.

"And how are we this week, Countess Vronsky?" asked Sam politely, as she dropped four quarters into his outstretched palm.

"Thriving, my dear, ever thriving. I hope the print of the film is not too scratchy." She adjusted her pince-nez.

"Not scratchy at all, Countess. In perfect condition."

"Did you happen to catch *Gunga Din* at the Garrick Theatre last week?"

"No, Countess."

"Very scratchy." She tightened her grip on the November 1917 issue of *Photoplay* she always carried with her, and swept past Sam.

Where do they come from? Where do they go? What causes these people to immerse their lives, their souls, their very existence in the never-never land of movie-star worship? Why do they tremble at the mention of the name Colleen Moore, go into paroxysms of ecstasy at the mention of the name Marguerite de la Motte, giggle with joy when someone can tell them the cast of *Wonder of Women,* MGM, 1929. Leila Hyams! Lewis Stone! Peggy Wood! How did you know, how did you know, how did you know!

"Sam!" snapped the little baldheaded man in the doorway. "What's with that goddam Museum of Modern Art? Why can't we get them to do an Isabel Jewell retrospective?"

"I'll look into it for you, Mr. Gordon," said Sam blandly.

"I'd appreciate it if you would. Good evening, Countess. I knew you wouldn't miss this show."

The big fat boy in his late twenties wore a black armband on his jacket.

"Not your mother!" said Sam with genuine concern.

"No, not Mummy," said the big fat boy, choking back the tears. "Zachawy Scott."

The back of the rented chauffeur-driven Cadillac rang with uproarious laughter as it headed toward East Fifty-sixth Street.

"Cat!" yelped Madeleine with delight as she patted Pharoah's hand, nestled snugly on her knee, where she had placed it three minutes ago. "You're a riot!" To Seth, "Why've you kept him hidden these past five months? He's not your bastard son, is he?"

They screamed with laughter again. The excellent

French dinner and the excellent French wines had done their job well.

"Why didn't we pick up Sweet Harriet and the Fleur sisters?" roared Seth.

"What!" yelled Madeleine. "And ruin my entrance?"

More uproar.

"Say," said Madeleine in a moment of calm, "I hope Sam knows he's not starting this screening on time. Us girls will be jockeying for entrance positions for *hours!*"

Nellie won't believe a word of this, thought the chauffeur, not a word of it. Her precious Madeleine Cartier digs niggers.

"Ready, pet?" boomed Flora.

"Just about," whispered Fauna.

"Head up. Chin out. Eyes wide. Forward march!"

Arm in arm they entered the building, heading toward the ground-floor auditorium where Sam Wyndham stood collecting dollars and wondering if he'd have to add extra chairs for tonight's performance.

"Girls! Girls!" beamed Sam, hands outstretched in greeting, revealing arms too short for the long, bony body that was topped by a squat head with hollow cheeks and thinning gray hair.

"Good evening, Samuel," whispered Fauna.

"Looks like a sellout, Sammy! Wonder if Jack Warner would stand up and salute if he knew we were still box-office?" Flora's hearty laugh cascaded into the auditorium, tapping each member of the audience on the shoulder. In a body the movie buffs rose, applauding with heartfelt generosity. Flora waved and Fauna smiled, and Lad, A Dog came trotting forward to lead them to the seats especially reserved for the guests of honor.

"Where's the other two?" Flora whispered in an aside to Sam.

"Not here yet. We'll give them a few more minutes."

The cab driver stared at his fare as she stood on the street rummaging in a large white purse.

"What does it say on the meter?" she squeaked.

"One dollar," said the cabbie, "just like it was two seconds ago."

"Here!" she piped, handing him a bill. "And this," extracting a postcard, "is for you."

She clickety-clacked into the building as the cab driver stared at the dimpled photograph on the postcard, at the bottom of which was written in a childish scrawl, "Ever thine, Sweet Harriet Dimple."

"Piss on you, lady," muttered the cab driver, tossing the photograph out the window and driving off.

Inside the auditorium, Flora and Fauna gaily signed autographs.

"You're just wonderful on those commercials," said the big fat boy, "better even than Jane Withers!"

"Isn't Sweet Harriet coming?" someone asked Flora.

"Wild dogs couldn't keep her away," boomed Flora. "She wouldn't miss this for—"

> *Tippy-tap-toe, tippy-tap-toe,*
> *My favorite da-a-a-ance.*
> *Tippy-tap-toe, tippy-tap-toe,*
> *Come on! Take a cha-a-a-ance!"*

Sam closed his eyes and counted slowly as Sweet Harriet came tap-dancing down the hallway, pirouetted and shot past him into the auditorium, landing with right knee bent forward, left leg extended straight out behind her, and right hand pointing at the assemblage, who were on their feet applauding and whistling.

Fauna stared at Flora, the two an isolated little island now, abandoned by their fickle fans for the new novelty who displayed herself before them and was generously awarded with thunderous applause.

"It's like I said, honey," muttered Flora, "you gotta hand it to the kid. She makes David Merrick look like a shrinking violet."

Seth stood on the sidewalk, watching Pharoah assist Madeleine from the Cadillac. One day, cat, thought Seth, you might master the fine art of underplaying.

"*Thank* you, kind sir," said Madeleine with a curtsy, her index finger holding up her chin.

"Shall I go inside and see if the other three have arrived yet?" asked Seth.

"The hell with it," said Madeleine. "Flora and Fauna are always early, and as for Sweet Harriet . . . " she left the sentence hanging in mid-air with a shrug.

Sam sighed with relief as he saw Madeleine coming down the hall followed by Seth and Pharoah. He left his post at the door and went to greet Madeleine with outstretched hands.

"Hello, honey! Thanks for coming."

"Hello, Sammy dear." She pecked his cheek swiftly and then turned to Seth and Pharoah. "This is Seth Piro." They shook hands. "And his friend, Pharoah Love. Enchanting name, isn't it? Reminds me of *Siren of the Nile*. Wouldn't he have made a marvelous Im-Ho-Tep instead of that hermaphrodite I had to play opposite?"

"Welcome, gentlemen," said Sam. Then to Seth, "We have a date to make, don't we? How's about after the screening?"

"Fine," said Seth.

"Follow me," said Sam. "You just missed Sweet Harriet's entrance."

"Not 'Tippy-Tap-Toe' again," sighed Madeleine.

"With a smash finish. Wait here and I'll introduce you." Sam entered the auditorium. "Ladies and gentlemen!" he shouted. "May I have your attention!"

Sweet Harriet went right on signing autographs.

"Here she is!" cried Sam. "*Miss* Madeleine *Cartier!*"

Madeleine swept into the room, arms outstretched à la Hildegarde, bejeweled neck, fingers and wrists dimmed only by the magic of her most enchanting smile, and bedlam reigned. The deafening applause was generously sprinkled with loud whistles and screams as Madeleine stood blowing kisses and bowing.

Sweet Harriet sank into the seat next to Flora and stared straight ahead at the blank screen on the platform at the far end of the room.

"Smile, dear," whispered Flora out of the side of her mouth to Sweet Harriet, "you're on Candid Camera."

Sam lead Madeleine, Seth and Pharoah to their seats as the buffs crowded around Madeleine for autographs. Sam shut the door to the auditorium, crossed to the rear of the room and checked the two sixteen-millimeter projectors, then made his way past the throng milling about Madeleine to the platform up front.

He stood on the platform with hands upraised. "Ladies and Gentlemen! Let's settle down, please. Please—take your seats. We're running a little late."

Slowly and reluctantly the buffs dispersed, and seats creaked and banged as rumps settled into them.

Sam smiled. "Welcome again, and welcome especially to the four *great* stars who have honored us with their presence tonight."

Applause.

Sam raised his hands for silence.

"Actually, I have another surprise in store for you, but that will have to wait until after the screening. I'm borrowing a bit from Hitch tonight" (laughter) "and adding a little suspense to the proceedings. Our program tonight is *Barclay Mill's Follies of 1932*, his last film, completed a few days before his—er—untimely death."

Flora took Fauna's hand and held it tightly. Sweet Harriet wondered who this colored man was sitting next to her. Probably the house dick at Madeleine's hotel. Wouldn't put it past that nymphomaniac. Madeleine felt as though every eye behind her was boring into the back of her neck. Seth snatched a quick look at her and saw a serene smile on the lovely face. Pharoah turned to Sweet Harriet, caught her eye and winked. Sweet Harriet lowered her head demurely. Couldn't be that Senegalese she was banging in Africa on that U.S.O. tour. He's either dead by now or in the U.N.

"We have an extremely fine print tonight." Applause. "And no scratches, Countess." Laughter. Inside joke,

Madeleine decided. "Our aging projectors are still a bit shaky, but I have some delightful news for you. A dear friend is donating two new projectors to our society. How can we express our thanks to—Sweet Harriet Dimple!"

Applause and cheers, and Sweet Harriet stood up and waved. Puzzled, Seth looked at Madeleine. She was clutching her purse tightly, biting her lower lip, her face red with fury. Fauna sat with head lowered and eyes closed, and Flora's face was granitely impassive as she flexed the fingers of her large hands. Sweet Harriet moved to sit down, and as she did her eyes locked with Madeleine's. Sweet Harriet puckered up her lips in a simulated kiss, then settled back in her seat, legs crossed, body tingling with triumph.

Sam had moved to the back of the auditorium, where he controlled the light switch and ran the projectors. With a flick of his finger he plunged the auditorium into darkness. As the first projector began to roll, a blare of trumpets emanated from the sound track, and on the screen flashed "A Smollett Brothers Presentation," followed by "Barclay Mill's Follies of 1932" to a brassy studio-orchestra accompaniment of a medley of the film's tunes.

The door to the auditorium opened and two latecomers entered. They were the same height, wore matching suits, and found two seats in the rear near the projectors.

"Just in time, Peter."

"Lucky us, Robert."

5

PETER AND ROBERT settled back in their seats and watched the credits of *Barclay Mill's Follies of 1932* unfold.

"Produced and Directed by Barclay Mill."

Thunderous applause.

"Original Story and Screenplay by Thurston Figg, Aurelia Gregson, Martin Thermaldi and Windston Trevor Pfifer-Drake."

One guffaw and several titters.

"Additional Scenes and Dialogue by Barclay Mill."

Thunderous applause.

"Entire Production Conceived and Staged by Barclay Mill."

Applause, thunder petering out.

The technical credits followed, segueing into a montage of shots of the featured players.

First, Sweet Harriet (By Christ, she was sweet, thought Seth) blew a kiss at her invisible audience. Under her chin was lettered "Sweet Harriet Dimple as Trixie Tracy."

Next, Fauna and Flora pirouetted into view and met center screen, laughing at the invisible audience with arms interlaced. (Were they ever that young and beautiful? mused Seth.) Across their bosoms was lettered "Fauna and Flora Fleur as Daisy and Maisie LaVerne."

There were oohs, ahs and squeals of delight from Sam Wyndham's audience when the face of the singing juvenile, Rick Drew, flashed on the screen. There he stood in his curly-haired, cleft-chinned glory, favoring the invisible ladies of the audience with a wink. Across his chest was lettered "Rick Drew as Tommy Trawlor."

Rick Drew segued to the suave, mustached good looks of the celebrated character actor Pat Warren. Applause. "Pat Warren as Nelson Vanderbilt III."

A bathing beauty on a diving board replaced Pat Warren. There was friendly applause before her identification appeared. As she poised to dive: "Zelma Wave as Winnie LePew." Zelma dived into the water, the camera panning with her.

As the waters into which Zelma disappeared settled down, there was superimposed on the screen "And Introducing Madeleine Cartier as Boots Bergdorf."

From out of the watery depths, head lowered on her bosom demurely, hands held stiffly at her side, Madeleine emerged on an invisible pedestal ("What an entrance!" Seth whispered, and Madeleine squeezed his hand), then slowly turned to the invisible audience and smiled her enchanting smile.

Thunderous applause, several appreciative whistles, and Pharoah wished Sweet Harriet would stop squirming in her seat.

Fade out.

Fade in.

Interior of a New York theater during the rehearsal of what was presumably a forthcoming musical extravaganza. To one side of the stage, piano and rehearsal pianist.

"It looks like Oscar Levant!" Seth heard someone behind him whisper excitedly.

"Nonsense!" (Countess Vronsky.) "It's Slavko Thomashevski."

"Quiet *please!*" (Lad, A Dog.)

In the center of the stage lit by a solitary overhanging fixture, Sweet Harriet Dimple, wearing rehearsal clothes —blouse and abbreviated pants—was singing with great gusto and lots of movement. Arms waving, legs clickety-clacking, croquignoles tossing.

"Keep your chin up, America,
We're coming out of the slump!

Hey, Mr. Stockbroker up on the roof,
Roll up your sleeves but don't jump!"

Big close-up of Sweet Harriet.

"Keep your chin up, America . . ."

Where was that sixty-piece orchestra coming from?

"We're getting a big new deal!"

What's that one-hundred-voice female chorus suddenly blending with Sweet Harriet on the soundtrack?

"Prosperity's just around the corner,
And they tell us we're getting Repeal!"

Magic! It's magic!

There was a long shot now, and, miracle of miracles, gone was the bare stage, gone were the blouse and abbreviated pants. Sweet Harriet was marching down Broadway twirling a golden, glittering baton with her left hand, carrying a blazing torch in her right, on her head a bejeweled crown, her costume a shimmering replica of the Statue of Liberty. Behind her marched one hundred chorus girls dressed like Uncle Sam, but beardless. The sidewalks were lined with a thousand cheering extras dressed in rags and selling apples.

"Throw away them apples . . ."

Apples flew in all directions and miraculously missed Sweet Harriet and the chorus.

"Laugh at Old Man Trouble!"

Quick montage of the bedraggled extras laughing hysterically.

"As old Ben Franklin used to say . . ."

Quick superimpose of Ben Franklin over the screen.

"It's Guy Kibbee!" Seth heard someone behind him whisper excitedly.

"Nonsense," (Countess Vronsky.) "It's Claude Gillingwater."

"Quiet, *please*." (Lad, A Dog.)

"Trouble's . . just . . a . . . bubbbbble!"

Bubbles burst all over the screen.

Overhead shot as Sweet Harriet and the chorus began to move into an intricate pattern to the orchestra's marching beat.

"Keep your chin up, America . . ."

The intricate pattern was beginning to look familiar.

"The big bad wolf's on the lam!"

Yes, yes, thought Seth, that's who it is.

"Keep your chin up, Amer-i-caaaaaaa . . ."

The pattern was completed and the Film Society audience in a body yelped with delight and applauded spontaneously.

"Put your trust in Uncle Sa-a-a-a-a-ammmm!"

Sweet Harriet and the one hundred chorus girls were a perfect replica of Uncle Sam, with Sweet Harriet emerging from his right eye and waving at the camera.

Two soporific reels later, with Madeleine yet to make her entrance, Seth's thoughts wandered to the file marked "Barclay Mill: Confidential."

Statement given to the police by Sweet Harriet Dimple:

Barclay had offered to lend me these here French books. You know, big boys. How to Speak French and all that, as I had this offer to make a movie in French in Paris, and I thought it was a good idea to learn the lingo, if you catch my drift. I offered to come for them right after dinner but he said no I shouldn't because he had a dinner guest and I should come around ten by which time his dinner guest would be gone as his dinner guest had an early call at the studio next day. No I did not know whom his dinner guest was as Barclay is very tight-lipped about them things. So around ten o'clock I am ringing the doorbell of his vast estate in Bel Air and after five minutes I think it's kind of funny the butler hasn't answered the door, unless Barclay gave him and the other ten servants the night off as he sometimes did when he was having a dinner guest if you catch my drift. So I tried the door and it was open. I went straight into the dining room but there was nobody there and the table wasn't even set or anything —you know, no dirty dishes or candles because he likes to eat by candles. So I think he is on the up-stairs terrace where he often goes to meditate and think up routines—for the dance numbers if you catch my drift. So I go back to the hall—no I didn't notice anything peculiar—and go up the stairs and to his bedroom which leads to the upstairs terrace. And there I saw the mess. Chairs and lamps over-turned and the bed all rumpled and the drapes torn off the hooks and the windows in the doors leading to the terrace all smashed but no Barclay. So I yelled Barclay Barclay where are you and naturally there was no answer if you catch my drift. So I run out on the terrace and there is still no Barclay and this fear grips my heart and a cold chill hits my spine. Like a magnet I was drawn to the edge of the terrace and I look over. There he's laying on the stone steps below leading to the swimming pool. I screamed. I ran down the steps at the side of the terrace which leads below and rush to his body. His head was all twisted lopsided and I screamed and screamed and then ran to the phone and called the police, knowing I will now never make that movie in French.

Tchaikovsky's *Swan Lake*.

Seth's eyes became riveted on the screen as Madeleine Cartier suddenly appeared in medium shot, dressed like a cygnet in white eiderdown, arms billowing gracefully as she toe-danced through a field of daisies toward a lake in the background. (Applause, and Madeleine was squeezing his hand again.) Rick Drew's treacly tenor filled the sound track as the camera panned with Madeleine toward the lake. Someone had provided Rick with lyrics set to *Swan Lake*.

> *"I saw you dancing near Swan Lake*
> *And lost my heart to lovely you."*

Now Zelma Wave appeared, dressed in an eiderdown bathing suit and an eiderdown bathing cap with an eiderdown wing over each ear, standing on a rock with arms outstretched, poised to dive.

> *"I saw you dive into Swan Lake . . ."*

Zelma shot into space and jackknifed into the water.

> *"And sink beneath the turquoise blue."*

The camera apparently dived into the water with Zelma and recorded an interminable underwater ballet featuring Madeleine as a mermaid, with another hundred mermaids sitting on rocks combing long blond wigs with shells.

Statement given to the police by Fauna Fleur:

> Barclay and I were to be married. We were keeping it a secret because—because, well, it seems that somewhere there was a Mrs. Barclay Mill. No. I had never known this before. I had never even sus-

pected. Barclay never discussed his private life. He asked me to have dinner with him that night, though he knew I had an early call at the studio the next morning. No. It wasn't one of Barclay's films. He was due to start one in a month. This is—this was to be my first starring role on my own. You know. By myself. Without my sister. Without anyone. Just me. We agreed to eat early as I wanted to be home in bed by nine, since I had to be at the studio at seven for make-up. Barclay was alone when I arrived at seven, as he had dismissed the servants. We decided to have a sort of picnic dinner and ate in the kitchen, which is sort of big for a picnic, as you have seen yourself. That's when he told me he was already married. Naturally, I didn't have much appetite when he told me that. But he kept insisting he loved me and only me and I believed him because he didn't have much appetite either. Of course I cried a lot at first and got angry and asked him to give me back all my letters but he kept saying I mustn't be a child and my letters were very dear to him though my handwriting was terrible. Anyway, I guess I seemed so upset, Barclay phoned my sister Flora to come get me. No, he couldn't drive me home himself as he was expecting Sweet Harriet Dimple who was coming to borrow some French grammars. No I was not jealous as Sweet Harriet and I are very good friends and I knew all about her romance with Barclay which had been over months ago. While waiting for Flora, Barclay kept begging me to stop crying as my eyes would be all red and puffy and they might not be able to shoot my close-ups. Finally Flora arrived and I told her Barclay was already married and she called him a four-letter word that begins with *f* which made me cry all the harder. And then Flora took me home and it couldn't have been more than eight o'clock as it is only a ten-minute drive from Barclay's estate to our mansion and I don't think I had been with him more than half an hour from the time I arrived and the time Flora came to take me home. And once we came home we stayed home because we now had a lot to talk about. Then Sweet Harriet phoned and told us what had happened and I got hysterical again. That's all I remember.

Laughter pounded at the walls of the auditorium, and Seth concentrated on the screen again. He had been completely oblivious to the finish of the underwater ballet.

Flora and Fauna now held center screen, playing a familiar concerto on twin grand pianos. Another dozen bars and Seth realized the concerto was a symphonic arrangement of "Tippy-Tap-Toe." The camera pulled back, and Flora and Fauna were on a vast sound stage surrounded by one hundred chorus girls pounding away at one hundred grand pianos, being pushed into intricate patterns by invisible hands. Suddenly, the one hundred and two grand pianos formed one huge grand piano (yelps of joy and tumultuous applause), and from the top of the screen, teeth clamped around what might have been a piano wire, Sweet Harriet ascended into view, then opened her mouth and landed feet first in the center of the huge grand piano, singing "Tippy-Tap-Toe."

Statement given to the police by Flora Fleur (with a note in parentheses that the suspect had been terribly uncooperative at first and had threatened to "belt" the interrogating officer):

Listen, flatfoot, don't ask me to tell you what was going on in Barclay Mill's mind, unless he happened to be looking at some skirt, and then it was obvious. No I was not jealous of my sister. No I did not want her to marry him. Because Barclay was okay to have an affair with but not to marry. Because I was told he's a satire, that's why! Listen stupid, that's a man who's always banging broads. Yeah, he and I did it a couple of times but that's water under the bridge. It was three years ago, back in 'twenty-nine. No, I wasn't in love with him, I wanted to get Fauna and me into pictures. Sure I wrote him letters. After we got the contract, I didn't have to any more. What do you mean, have to what? Bang or write! Besides, I was getting too old for him. None of your damn business how old! By him, anything over sixteen was old. Besides, he had met Sweet Harriet. Sure he used to get depressed a lot. Don't all geniuses? How should I know if he's the suicidal type? What's a suicidal type? Of course he must have had enemies. No I never threatened to kill him. No! Not even the night he died. I was too worried about Fauna. When Barclay phoned me to come get her I was listening to the radio. Harry Horlick and the A and P Gypsies. When I got there they were in the kitchen and Fauna was blubbering into some cold chicken salad. I didn't ask what she was blubbering about because she was in no shape to talk. I just called Barclay a dirty old fuck and took Fauna home. At home I gave her a nerve pill. She takes nerve pills for her nerves, goddammit, what do you think she takes nerve pills for, hangnails? The nerve pills calm her, that's what they do. So anyway, once she was becalmed, she told me Barclay had a wife stashed away someplace and I can tell you right here and now I had a good mind to go back there! You said yourself he was killed sometime between nine and nine-thirty, and Fauna and me was home then. Just ask Fauna. And besides, Madeleine Cartier came over to spend the night with us because she wasn't feeling so good and didn't want to be by herself. She was at the house waiting for us when Fauna and me got back from Barclay's. Well what do you think the three of us did? We got stoned! Say wait a minute, wise guy. The papers said this morning he committed suicide. What's with the "killed" bit all of a sudden? Okay Buster. Stay clammed up if you like. I can play potsy too. No tickee, no washee.

It was Madeleine's elbow Seth felt jabbing his ribs. The grand finale was being unreeled. Flora, Fauna,

Sweet Harriet, Madeleine, Zelma Wave and the other principals were lined up at the head of a gigantic marble staircase, dressed in sailor suits, behind them the one hundred chorus girls in an inevitable Barclay Mill arrangement as the American flag, shuffling backward and forward with impeccable timing to simulate the flag billowing in the breeze. The principals were bellowing with zest, fervor and sincerity as they high-kicked down the gigantic marble staircase toward the camera.

> *"Let's stick to-geth-er!*
> *To-geth-er we don't fall apart!*
> *Let's show the good old U.S.A.*
> *We've got heart! Heaaaaaart!"*

All down on their knees now, waving their fists like cheerleaders.

> *"Ziss . . . boom . . . bah!*
> *Ziss . . . boom . . . bah!*
> *U.S.A. has . . . heart! Heart!"*

Back on their feet and high-kicking.

> *"H–E–A–R–T–HEAAAAAAAAAART!"*

Six tiny letters came flying out from what was presumably Sweet Harriet's dimpled heart, until they filled the screen: "THE END."

Thunderous applause, cheers, whistles deafened Seth's ears as Sam Wyndham switched on the lights and crossed to the front of the auditorium, beaming from ear to ear. Peter and Robert exchanged glances as Sam passed them. Sam stood in front of the screen and gestured to Madeleine, Fauna, Flora and Sweet Harriet. Age may have withered them, but time had not dulled their reflexes. The four arose together, beaming grandly and waving to the faithful.

Pharoah caught Seth's eye and indicated Madeleine. Her right hand was growing limp and drifting lazily downward. The smile on her face had frozen as she stared at the rear of the auditorium. Seth and Pharoah swiveled their necks and saw Peter and Robert. Flora whispered something to Fauna, and her eyes focused on the twins. Sweet Harriet was blowing kisses.

"I have a surprise for all of you!" Sam was shouting over the din. "Settle down! I have a surprise for you!" The ladies sat, the ovation ended and Sam cleared his throat. "As I said before the screening, I have a surprise in store for you."

"Are you all right?" Seth whispered to Madeleine, who sat with her head lowered.

"I'm just dandy." Each word was like a poisoned dart.

"Barclay Mill's death was one of the great tragedies and unsolved mysteries in motion picture history," Sam was saying in his dry, pedantic delivery. "As you all know, I was close to Barclay for several years, having been chief cameraman on his four major productions. And even I never suspected there was a Mrs. Barclay Mill."

Fauna's voice was so faint, Flora had to strain to hear her. "We shouldn't have come."

Sweet Harriet demurely rearranged the pleats of her accordion skirt.

"But there *was* a Mrs. Barclay Mill, and—" he smiled slyly—"there was issue from the union." Archaic bastard, Madeleine thought to herself, he'll pay for this.

"And the issue," Sam droned, "is with us tonight!"

"Oh, God, no," Pharoah heard Madeleine whisper.

"Ladies and gentlemen," smiled Sam, "introducing Francis K. Mill!" And he gestured to the rear of the auditorium.

All heads turned, and the big fat boy with the black armband on his jacket sleeve stood up.

Seth studied him as he seemed to bask in the generous applause. At first his face resembled a cherubic infant's. Thirty seconds later Seth pegged the fat boy to be in his middle thirties.

"Thank you one and all," began Francis K. Mill in a voice as soft as his body.

"Speak up!" (Countess Vronsky.)

Francis K. cleared his throat. "Muthuh wanted to be here tonight, but she is confined to a wheelchair with pawalysis." Fat boy has trouble with his *r*'s. Pharoah stifled a giggle. "She sends you all her fondest wegahds."

Madeleine had not turned to look at Fat Boy. Her eyes were riveted on Sam Wyndham. Flora sat with her arms folded, contemplating the back of the seat in front of her. Fauna clutched her purse tightly and bit her lower lip.

Sweet Harriet demurely rearranged the pleats of her accordion skirt.

"Muthuh is now whiting huh memwahs with my assistance and will explain why huh mawiage to Daddy was kept a secwet, and why she chose to wemain anonymous aftuh his death. Mostly, of cawss, to pwotect me. Thank you."

Fat Boy beamed at the friendly applause as he sat down.

Madeleine mustered a smile as she turned to Seth. "Let's get out of here. And no questions. For God's sake, no questions!"

"I think your host and your co-stars were annoyed at your leaving without saying good night, Madeleine."

The limousine was headed west on Fifty-seventh Street. Pharoah lit a cigarette after Madeleine, with an impatient wave of her hand, refused the one he offered her.

Seth sighed and looked out the window. She had chosen to ignore his statement.

"What do you say, cats? Shall we head up to Ida's place for a drink?" Pharoah leaned forward, looking hopefully at his dour companions.

Seth patted Madeleine's hand. "A drink might do us all good."

Madeleine finally spoke, her voice sounding dull and musty, as though covered with a layer of dust. "Heavy, heavy hangs over my head."

"Who was Barclay Mill's wife?" asked Seth.

The traces of a wry smile began to play around Madeleine's mouth. "Who was the most unnecessary character in the movie you just saw?" she asked.

Seth was tempted to reply, "All of you," but instead he shrugged.

"Detective cat?" asked Madeleine with a touch of whimsy in her voice as she turned to Pharoah.

"You tell *me*," said Pharoah.

"The waterlogged beauty," sighed Madeleine, "Miss Breast Stroke of 1928. Zelma Wave."

6

"ZELMA WAVE!" exclaimed Seth.

"Well, who'd you think," sniffed Madeleine, "Rick Drew?"

"Have you known it was Zelma all this time?"

Cat, thought Pharoah, you do have a way with the lady.

Madeleine reached over and appropriated Pharoah's cigarette from between his index finger and thumb and took a deep drag on it.

"Zelma told me about it around three years after Barclay's murder. I was riding the crest of the wave then, and on my way to being a very rich lady. She was showing the first signs of the arthritis that eventually crippled her. Musicals had been out then for at least two years, and so was Zelma. Zelma had been very kind to me during the shooting of *Follies of '32*. She must have kept me from drowning at least three times during that damned *Swan Lake* number. Anyway, she'd been trying to get in touch with me for months, but apparently Sam had been intercepting her letters and her phone calls."

"Did Sam cat know she was the widow Mill?" asked Pharoah.

"He says he didn't. But the truth never came easily to our Samuel. Well, it just so happened that Sam had to go on location with some Western, and Zelma finally made contact with me. She looked a hundred years old. She couldn't have been more then twenty-five or twenty-six then. She asked me for a handout. Not so much for herself, but for her baby. . . ."

"Baby!"

Madeleine's voice echoed across the patio of her Beverly Hills estate. Zelma picked at a thread that hung from the sleeve of her too-often-laundered blouse.

"A boy," said Zelma softly. "Francis K."

"Just the initial *K?*" asked Madeleine incredulously, stirring her iced tea and wondering if she dare eat one of the chocolate-covered marshmallow biscuits.

"Yes," said Zelma. "If it had been a girl, I would have called him Kay Francis—" with a wistful smile—"my favorite actress. Since the baby turned out to be a boy, I just reversed it. Francis K." She drew an official-looking document from her purse. "Here's his birth certificate."

"I don't have to see it!" laughed Madeleine, right hand descending on a marshmallow biscuit. "I take your word for it."

"Read it," said Zelma, unfolding the birth certificate and holding it in front of Madeleine. Madeleine's mouth opened, but not to bite into the biscuit. It had dropped from her hand and lay on the ground, where the advance guard of an army of ants was already investigating its nutritional possibilities.

"Barclay Mill?" said Madeleine. "But, for crying out loud—when?"

"Back in 'twenty-eight," said Zelma, "when he staged an aquacade I was starring in down in Florida. We were married June eleventh and I gave birth to Francis K. four days later. It took me that long to get Barclay to marry me. Fortunately, the aquacade was backed by a syndicate of gangsters who were very fond of me. They weren't very fond of Barclay, because my pregnancy forced them to close the show, especially when they couldn't get Gertrude Ederle to replace me. So Vito the Vulture—one of the boys—shoved a gun in Barclay's back and didn't remove it until we exchanged vows. Then Barclay got the Hollywood contract and made a deal with me to keep our marriage a secret. I wouldn't give him a divorce, because that would have meant losing whatever hold I had on him and his responsibility to the baby."

Madeleine stared at the pain-racked face. "Why didn't you come forward when Barclay was murdered?"

"And become the leading suspect?"

Madeleine nodded mechanically.

"I need money, Madeleine. I'm broke. When Barclay died, my income died with him. Even if he had left an estate, I couldn't dare make a claim on it. As it was, he was up to his ears in hock when he was murdered. You'll help me, won't you Madeleine."

It wasn't a request. It was a demand.

"You see," she continued, fidgeting with the clasp on her purse, "my only other alternative is to try and sell my story to a newspaper or a magazine, and that would mean reopening the whole mess again and . . ."

". . . And I paid her," said Madeleine flatly, handing the smoldering stub of the cigarette to Seth, who lowered a window and flipped the butt out.

"Francis K.," Madeleine snorted. "He even has trouble with his *r*'s the way Kay Francis did! Wouldn't you know," she added ruefully, "all my chickens would come home to roost now—now of all times?"

"Not that it matters much," said Pharoah, "but how much did aquatic cat clip you?"

"Don't ask how much, sweetie cat," purred Madeleine, "ask for how long. Until five years ago, when I was presumably out on my ear in pictures forever, at which point I wrote her and told her my cup no longer runneth over and little Francis K. must certainly be old enough to go out and earn a living for himself and Momma. I never heard from either of them after that—until tonight. So now Momma is 'whiting her memwahs.' Goody goody gumdrops. Where's this Ida's you were talking about? Let's go up and have that drink."

"Columbus Avenue in the Seventies," said Seth. The limousine nosed up Broadway toward Columbus.

"Madeleine," said Seth, "did you ever ask Zelma where she was the night Mill was murdered?"

"I didn't have to," said Madeleine. "I knew. She was making a personal appearance in San Francisco, after which she swam across the bay to Oakland and broke some goddamned record. She should have broken her goddamned neck."

Flora saw Seth and Pharoah make a flying wedge for Madeleine through the crowd at the door of the auditorium and cursed Madeleine under her breath for not having offered to drive Fauna and her home.

"I feel sick, Flora."

Flora put her arm around Fauna's waist, shoving people to one side as she assisted Fauna to the hall.

"Anything I can do, kiddo?" she heard Sweet Harriet ask.

"You can fuck yourself."

Sweet Harriet brushed some lint from her sleeve and then heard Sam Wyndham say to her, "You and I have to have a talk." She turned her head to him and spoke out of the side of her mouth. "Buzz me in the morning, big boy." And she lost herself in a circle of admirers.

"Peter."

"Yes, Robert."

They hadn't left their seats.

"I think we must request an audience with Zelma Wave."

"The fat thing is still here. Shall we surround him?"

"Physically an impossibility, but worth the try. We'll have to disengage him from yonder virago."

Francis K. was deep in conversation with Countess Vronsky.

"Arthritis!" exclaimed the Countess. "How sad! Has she tried the baths at Wiesbaden?"

"Mummy can't twavel," said Francis K. sadly. "She is twapped between bed and wheel chaiah."

"Mr. Mill, forgive us." The words embraced Francis K. and stroked his cheeks and kissed his ears.

Francis K. turned and stared at the beautiful twins he had noticed when the lights went up. He tried to pull in his stomach and smiled his most cherubic of cherubic smiles. "Oh, hello theah!"

"If the good lady will forgive this intrusion," spinet-toned Robert, "my brother and I would like a word with you."

Sam Wyndham watched Peter and Robert lead Francis K. to the far corner of the auditorium. Sam worried himself with a single thought. I overplayed my hand tonight. The new movie projectors were one thing, but inviting Francis K. was another. I've pushed Madeleine too far. Just a little too far. She won't pay for those machines. There was a click in his brain and the reels switched.

Where was Baby Lake Sturgeon and her crowd? She promised to bring some reporters and photographers. I could use some decent publicity. Screwy undependable broad. And why did that Piro guy rush Madeleine out of here without making a date for tomorrow? Or did Madeleine insist he get her out of here pronto? She's mad. Oh yes, she's mad. The hell with her. I've got a hold on her. I'll always have a hold on her. She'll jump when I snap my fingers. If I have to snap my fingers.

And why the hell did the twins decide to show up?

"Well!" exhaled Francis K., and Peter thought of holding on to Robert to keep from falling over. Such breath. "All I can do is ask Mummy. I mean huh memwahs ah one thing, but anothuh stowy about Daddy . . . Wheah can I weach you tomowwow?"

Robert handed him a slip of paper with a telephone number. "It's an answering service. Just leave a message. We'd appreciate your cooperation."

"Well!" chirruped Francis K., "I'll weally twy."

"Good night," said Robert.

"Nighty night."

"Good night," said Peter.

"Aw wevwah."

"Mr. Mill," cried Lad, A Dog, waving an album and fountain pen. "Can I have your autograph for my Mommy? He's bedridden, too."

"So we meet at last, Mr. Wyndham," said Peter.

"A charming evening," added Robert.

"Glad you could come," muttered Sam, glancing about furtively to make sure no one else was within earshot. "I thought I asked you both to wait till tomorrow."

"There's no time like the present," said Peter. "Can we give you a lift to your place?"

"I have a previous engagement," said Sam stonily. "Call me tomorrow, like I said." And he pushed his way past them in response to Countess Vronsky's beckoning finger.

"The beggar," snapped Peter.

"Temper," cautioned Robert. "Everything will fall in place—all in good time. We've waited this long. We can wait till tomorrow. Let's have a drink. That charming place on Columbus Avenue. Shall we favor it with our presence, Peter?"

"Lead on, Robert."

They passed Sweet Harriet on their way out and nodded.

"I said tomorrow, four o'clock, my hotel!" she snapped, and resumed signing autographs.

"Tomorrow and tomorrow and tomorrow . . ." intoned Peter as he followed his brother out.

The Frugers and Watusiers automatically made a path for Ida Maruzzi as she led Madeleine, Seth and Pharoah to a table. Her flaming red hair hung in an Alice-in-Wonderland style, with a huge polka-dot bow clipped at the back of it. Her bouncy and nimble gait belied her fifty years and her mammoth girth. Madeleine had liked her at once.

"Won't you join us?" asked Madeleine when the three were seated.

"Maybe later." Ida smiled, removing the cigar from her mouth as she spoke. "Have to keep an eye on the crowd for a while, and I'm breaking in a new bartender. I lost my last one to the bus-and-truck company of some *farshtunkener* comedy. Lester!" She snapped her fingers at a passing waiter. "Take the orders here. First round on the house."

"Champagne," purred Madeleine at her movie-star

best, and Lester wondered if he dare ask for an autograph.

"Double scotches for me and this cat," ordered Pharoah before Seth could move his lips. Madeleine was examining her face in her compact mirror.

"On the rocks," Seth added, and Lester nodded and left.

Madeleine snapped the compact shut, popped it into her purse, and placed the purse on the table at her elbow. She propped her elbows on the table and shored up her chin with the palms of her hands.

"Don't look so glum, Seth."

"I'm not glum. Just a little brain-weary."

"You're also annoyed with me. He *is* annoyed with me, isn't he, Pharoah cat? I mean, you probably know him better than anyone—isn't he annoyed with me?"

"Seth cat can talk for himself."

"Talk for yourself, Seth cat."

Seth took his time about lighting a cigarette, then directed his eyes at Madeleine.

"I was reminding myself you were going to dismiss Barclay Mill in your autobiography with just a few sentences."

Madeleine leaned back in her chair. "And exactly how much honesty do you find in most movie-queen autobiographies? Do you expect the girls to list their. abortions, their sexual aberrations, the physical beatings they've taken, the blackmail they've been subjected to, the pornography they once posed for? Mind you, I'm speaking in generalities. I'm not giving you a capsule summing up of the kid herself, though I've taken a few beatings and, as you now know, been blackmailed."

Seth blew a smoke ring and Pharoah poked his finger through it.

"Did you kill Barclay Mill?" It was Seth who spoke.

"No, dear, I did not." How easily she said it. Pharoah was impressed.

"Then who did?" asked Seth.

"I'm not a detective."

"Then whom are you protecting?"

"Myself."

"So what if Zelma Wave had revealed she was Barclay Mill's wife and the mother of his son? How could that have harmed you?"

"You have to remember this was thirty years ago. Barclay's death had almost finished my career three years earlier. I was still an impressionable kid. Zelma frightened me, that's all. Everything frightened me then."

"And nothing frightens you now?"

"Snakes, rodents, and sometimes the dark. Here are our drinks."

They sat in silence while Lester served the Scotches and poured the champagne.

"Joining us in Central Park tomorrow night, Pharoah cat?" Madeleine asked lightly. Seth couldn't recall if he had promised to be at the open-air concert featuring the music from Barclay Mill films. Madeleine detailed the program to Pharoah.

"I just might be there at that, actress cat," smiled Pharoah. "I can always use a little fresh air."

"Where did you say Sweet Harriet gets her money?" Seth again.

"From friends." Madeleine sipped her champagne.

"Enough to donate a pair of sixteen-millimeter projectors to Sam Wyndham?"

"Goddammit!"

Even Ida heard that one at the opposite end of the room. "Movie star," she said to a barfly's inquisitive look. Someone fed the jukebox and Lena Horne wondered why she was born.

"Dear dear dear," murmured Madeleine, "I can still project, can't I? Wherever he is, how Barclay must be chortling. A very nasty man, that. Very nasty." Then wearily, "I've been supporting Sweet Harriet for years. And she was *supposed* to have *stayed* in *Hollywood*. A lot of people have been on my payroll over the years, Seth *darling*, including my ex-husband." She drained the glass of champagne, and Pharoah refilled it. "Thank you, sweetie cat." To Seth, "Are you supposed to be ghosting my memoirs or trying to solve Barclay Mill's murder?"

"I'm not trying—"

"Yes you are!" she cut in with the swiftness of a whip. "You have the confidential file on the case from L.A." Pharoah's eyes were wide with astonishment. "I've got a friend or two on the L.A. force, too. I've been arrested often enough."

"It's part of my research," insisted Seth.

"Oh, I don't give a damn about the file," said Madeleine airily. "There's nothing there that hasn't been published except for one or two minor items. They don't even know how the newspapers got hold of all the love letters Barclay had been hoarding. Barclay, dear Barclay. You are certainly making one hell of a comeback even from beyond the grave. You know those twins you saw tailgating Sweet Harriet this afternoon?"

"I told him who they are," said Pharoah.

"And how do *you* know them?"

"Dropped in at the precinct today looking for some information."

"Then I suppose you know they're looking for Barclay Mill's murderer."

"I know they're doing a chapter on him for a book of unsolved Hollywood murders."

She leaned forward, almost tipping the glass of champagne. "That's only part of it, detective *cat*. They're looking for Barclay Mill's murderer."

Pharoah shrugged and Seth drummed on the table with his fingers, his Scotch still strangely untouched.

"Don't you remember them?" she asked softly. "From pictures, when they were kids? The Moulin twins?"

"Hot damn!" cried Pharoah. "I *thought* they looked familiar!"

"They were *good,* too," said Madeleine warmly. "Chips off the old blocks."

"Which old blocks?" asked Seth.

"Ohhhh," said Madeleine, "mother and father were small-part players in pictures. Killed in an auto crash or something when the kids were infants, and they grew up in a home for orphaned children—something like that. Don't you remember that picture I did with the boys?"

Seth wondered if he would ever see Madeleine's face aglow again so ethereally. *"Stella's Children,"* Madeleine told them, "the biggest tear-jerker of its day. One of my really *biiiiig* smash hits. It was their first picture. We hunted for months for twin boys. And I found them in the orphanage. They were so adorable. So smart. So . . ."

She stared past Seth at the entrance.

"And, like someone would inevitably say in every Barclay Mill musical—here they are now."

7

PETER AND ROBERT stood in the entrance, and two doz-
en women and six men caught their breath. Peter and
Robert's eyes swiftly swept across the room like kleig
lights at a Hollywood opening.

"I see Miss Cartier," said Robert.

"And friends," added Peter.

"I told you no more questions." Ida stood in front of
them, hands on hips, a general defending her fortress.
How Rubens could have immortalized her, thought Robert. Robert's lips parted in the smile.

"At the moment, we ask only for libations."

"Translate," snapped Ida.

"We want a drink," clarified Peter.

Lester arrived and spoke to the twins. "Miss Cartier
would like you to join her party."

"How kind," said Robert. Peter winked at Ida as he
and his twin followed Lester to the far side of the room.

Ida motioned to another waiter. "Tell Seth I have to talk
to him when he gets a minute. And don't let the others
hear you."

"You've already met Mr. Love," said Madeleine, out-
bubbling the champagne. "This is Seth Piro. Seth . . .
Peter and Robert Moulin."

Seth shook hands with the twins as Lester confiscated
two chairs from an adjoining table. By the time the twins
were settled, Ida's message had been delivered to Seth,
and Lester was on his way to the bar for daiquiris on the
rocks.

"Are you enjoying New York, darlings?" asked Madeleine as Pharoah refilled her glass.

"It's rather amusing," said Robert, eyeing a stain on the tablecloth with disapproval.

"Loved tonight's flick," Peter said to Madeleine. "So innocent, so charmingly naïve. Weren't they all magnificent, Mr. Love? Would you have guessed one of them was capable of murder?"

"*Must* we talk about murder?" Madeleine asked petulantly.

"Murder," said Peter, "like the rich, is always with us. Isn't that so, Mr. Piro?"

"According to statistics, there is one murder a day committed in New York." Seth sounded as though he had memorized an official brochure.

"One a day," repeated Peter. "Sounds like one of those vitamin pills we've seen Fauna Fleur hawking on television. Been involved in any good murders since the Ben Bentley case, Mr. Love?"

"Seth cat," observed Pharoah, "you're sloshing your drink." Then he fixed Peter with a benign expression in his eyes. "There's nothing good about murder."

"It's even worse," offered Robert, "when the murderer escapes justice." Seth took a a long swig of his Scotch.

"I was a murderess once," said Madeleine richly. Lester was taking his time about serving the daiquiris. He was hoping to hear the rest of Madeleine's statement. She swiftly obliged. "One of my biggest flops. 'Lady X.' I committed murder in that one to defend my daughter's honor. I thought it would break everyone's heart. Unfortunately," she said grimly, raising her glass toward Pharoah for another refill, "at the première there wasn't a wet eye in the house. Waiter! Another bottle!" Lester departed reluctantly.

"Take the murder of Mr. Bentley." Peter savored each word like a toasted peanut. "In your book, Mr. Piro, you paint such a sympathetic portrait of the young Indian, Adam Littlestorm, one finds it difficult to believe him capable of homicide. And yet you manage to state the case against him so convincingly. Robert and I frequently find ourselves sympathizing with the murderers in the cases we reconstruct."

"Frequently," said Robert after a sip of his daiquiri, "especially when we suspect there's been a miscarriage of justice."

Pharoah took aim and fired. "If Adam Littlestorm didn't kill Ben Bentley, who do you cats think did?"

Robert loaded and pointed his mouth at Pharoah. "Peter didn't say Mr. Piro's deduction was incorrect. Only that we found it difficult to believe the Indian capable of homicide. You see, we feel that Mr. Bentley's murder was a crime of passion, and throughout Mr. Piro's book Mr. Littlestorm's attitude toward the victim seems dispassionate, although we eventually learn Mr. Bentley was attempting to blackmail him."

Seth had drained his glass and was grateful for Lester's return. "To quote Oliver Twist," Seth said, lifting the empty glass, "more, please."

"And me," added Pharoah.

They didn't succeed in derailing Robert's train of thought.

"Now, do correct or amend if I'm wrong, Mr. Piro. You were in the bathroom with Mr. Bentley shortly before he was done in. He is sitting in the tub, caroling in accompaniment to the radio on a shelf at least two feet above his head. You tell him you are basing your new book on his nefarious activities as a professional whore. It's logical to assume an argument might have erupted between you and in a fit of passionate fury you found something with which to strike him—the radio, for example—thereby electrocuting the poor bugger, water being such a tiresome conductor of electricity."

Pharoah was amazed at the steadiness of Seth's voice when he spoke. "Research men can be such tiresome conductors of incorrect deductions."

"You are so *right!*" laughed Peter, his foot gently connecting with Robert's shin under the table as Lester delivered the fresh round of drinks. "Take the murder of Barclay Mill. In the past six months we've arrived at and discarded at least a dozen possible solutions."

"Oh, forget the damn case!" exploded Madeleine. "Go back to California and *forget* the damn case."

75

"But, Madeleine," said Robert softly, "Peter and I are committed."

"Yes, you are, aren't you?" sighed Madeleine, the words slightly slurred. "You most certainly are. Oh, you babies! You poor, dear babies! Still tying tin cans to sleeping dogs! Don't get bitten, my darlings, don't get bitten! I want to dance." She waved her hands gaily, and Pharoah was tempted to applaud the brilliant transition. "Dance with me, somebody. Dance with me, Robert." She was out of her chair and tugging at Robert's arm.

Ida was grinding the butt of her cigar into the sawdust. Though Madeleine's cheek was pressed tightly against Robert's, Ida could see her lips moving. Occasionally Robert's lips moved in reply. Cool, thought Ida, real cool.

The lips that touched her cheek felt feverish. Ida turned to Seth and spoke swiftly.

"That one"—indicating Robert with a subtle jerk of her head—"and his carbon copy were in here earlier and trying to pump. You. Pharoah. Ben Bentley. The works. Well, you might try acting surprised."

"Why be surprised?" said Seth lazily. "I have an appointment in Samarra." He pinched her cheek and returned to the table.

"Hey, you," snapped Ida to Lester, "where's Samarra?"

"I think it's near Poughkeepsie," said Lester, and he disappeared with a loaded tray.

"Who were you talking to?" asked Fauna weakly as Flora entered the bedroom.

"Did you take your pill?"

"You're trembling. Who were you talking to?"

"Go to sleep."

Fauna sat up, clutching the bedcover to her chest. "Who was it, Flora?"

"Jesus T. Eloise Christ!" stormed Flora. "Go to sleep!"

Fauna settled back slowly onto the pillow. Flora lit a cigarette and sat on the edge of her bed.

"What are you wearing tomorrow night?" she asked Fauna.

"Whatever you say."

"Yeah—whatever I say." Her sigh made the curtains quiver. "Whatever I say."

"Go, girl, go!"
"Let 'er rip, baby! Let 'er rip!"

> *"Kick up your heels, kick up your toes,*
> *Slap your backside and thumb your nose,*
> *Everybody do the Sorority Stomp!"*

"Mama mia! Mama mia!" Ida clasped her hands and stared at the ceiling in supplication. Madeleine was dancing on a table, hair disarrayed, hands waving wildly over her head, belting as she hadn't belted in thirty years. The crowd roared its approval and shouted encouragement, and Madeleine let it rip. Seth tried to gauge her weight in case she fell in his direction. The twins clutched opposite ends of the table to keep it from tipping. Pharoah stood to one side, arms folded, one hand clutching his third double Scotch.

Twin cats, he was thinking, your claws need clipping. You've been taking cat swipes at Seth baby cat, and though it isn't visible to the naked eye you've drawn blood. Just minor wounds, and they'll heal, but claws get sharper and gashes can get deeper and sometimes they can make guts spill. Not Seth cat's guts, twin cats, not Seth cat's guts. We are not twins, Peter cat and Robert cat, but we are One. We are attached at a vital organ. The soul. Separate Seth cat from me and we both die. I'm going to clip your claws.

The room reverberated with roars of approval and appreciation as Madeleine blew kisses, then somewhat unsteadily extended her hand to Seth, who helped her down from the table. She grabbed his ears and pulled his mouth to hers. Peter and Robert smiled at Pharoah (little cat smiles), and he winked in return.

"Wow wow wow," wowed Madeleine, "I haven't danced on a table since the good old days at the Cocoanut Grove. Hey, Ida! It's hot in here. Smash the windows! Madame needs air. Champagne! Champagne for everybody! It's my party. I love you all. I love every single one of you. My public—my dear unpredictable, fickle public. Smile, Peter! Smile, Robert! Kiss me, Pharoah!" She leaped at him, missed his mouth, caught his chin, and his drink went trickling down the front of her dress.

Sam Wyndham was positive the clock was making faces at him. He blinked his eyes, but they refused to focus. He lifted the gin bottle to his lips and took three gulps, choking on the third. His eyes teared, his face grew redder and the bottle crashed to the floor. He sank into a chair, gasping for breath, and soon the coughing fit subsided.

"If I could only sleep," he said to the ghosts that shared his mean little apartment. "If I could only sleep. Why won't you let me sleep? I'm afraid. I'm afraid."

I'm afraid, I'm afraid, I'm afraid. The words bounced off the walls and struck back at him.

"Madeleine!" he shrieked. "Madeleine!" Then he closed his eyes and passed out.

Madeleine sat between Peter and Robert with her arms around them. "My boys! My dear darling boys! They owe me everything! Don't you, boys?"

"We always pay our debts," crooned Peter.

"Hey, Pharoah cat!" (Pharoah cat wants to go home, Madeleine cat.) "Did you know these two kids are war heroes? Korea. My brave, brave babies. Who's been drinking up all my champagne? Hey, Ida! Send over another bottle."

"Madeleine," said Seth, "it is very late."

"Seth angel sweetie cat lover baby doll, it is later than you think. Champagne! Champagne! Champagne!"

"She's dead drunk," Lester agonized to Ida.

"Show her the bill," said Ida listlessly. "That'll sober her up."

"But it's too late, Mummy! It's too late! I told the whole woom full of people about the memwahs!"

The haggard, pain-racked face stared across the kitchen table at the fat boy.

"Tomorrow," said Zelma Wave, the wheel chair creaking as she looked down at her gnarled fingers, "tomorrow you must phone Madeleine Cartier. I have to see her. I have to talk to her. She was good to us, Frannie sweetheart, she was always good to us. A real good friend." Her voice hardened. "I don't want her for an enemy. I won't see anyone but Madeleine. You hear me, Frannie?"

Francis K. began wringing his hands. "But what about Petah and Wobbit? I *pwomised* them."

"Now, you listen to me, damn you!"

"All wight, Mummy, all wight. Shall I wheel you to the bedwoom?"

"What time is it?"

"It's past thwee."

"Go to bed."

"But, Mummy!"

"Go to bed, I said."

"Yes, Mummy."

Zelma watched him leave the room, shaking her head in despair. I've got to straighten this out with Madeleine tomorrow. She mustn't think I'm after money again. Frannie's taking care of me now. The shop does all right. There are plenty of customers for old movie magazines and old movie stills and old movie posters. I've got to straighten it out with Madeleine, because I'm afraid. One of those five murdered Barclay. It had to be one of those five. And one of those five will murder again. It mustn't be me. It mustn't be Frannie. Frannie! Oh, my poor baby. My poor chubby little brown-eyed baby. How I fought for your survival. How I lowered myself! Blackmail. I wasn't afraid then. I was young and I was desperate. I'm afraid now. I'm old and I'm desperate.

"I am *not* drunk!" yelped Madeleine, slapping Seth's hands away.

79

"You were about to fall off the chair," Seth insisted.

"G'wan. You were just making a pass at me. Wasn't he, Pharoah cat?"

"I didn't notice, actress cat."

"Wasn't he, Robert cat?"

"I don't think so, Madeleine cat."

"Peter cat?"

"It's almost four in the morning, my dear," was Peter's response. "Can't we take you home? Have to look all pretty and pert for tomorrow night's concert, don't you?"

"Memoirs." The word slid out of her mouth like a message slipped under a door. "Ev-ree-bod-ee's writin' duh memoirs!" Jimmy Durante would have winced. "Why does everybody keep picking on me?" She burst into tears.

The room was empty except for Ida, the bartender and the five at Madeleine's table. "Hey, gang," shouted Ida, "time to close." She studied the one-hundred dollar bill Madeleine had given her and hoped it wasn't counterfeit.

"Who's yelling?" sobbed Madeleine.

"Ida," said Seth. "She wants us to go home."

"Ida baby angel sweet Texas Guinan Heaven, come over here and sit down!" Madeleine wiped her eyes with an edge of the tablecloth, and when she was finished Ida was sitting between Seth and Pharoah.

"Ida"—the tone of Madeleine's voice was meant to wring every last drop of pathos from everyone present— "woman to woman, do you think I'm a nymphomaniac?"

"Shit, woman, I can't even spell it."

"I had such a rotten childhood. And they had a rotten childhood"—pointing at Peter and Robert—"and the older I got it didn't get any better. Men always violated me. The only really good thing I ever did in my life was get those two kids out of the orphanage and into the Screen Actors' Guild. And are they grateful? The hell they are! They won't let Barclay Mill rest in peace! Rest in peace, you son of a bitch"—waving a fist at the ceiling—"rest in peace! You may as well. Nobody else can."

"Peter."

"Yes, Robert."

"I suspect her stream of consciousness is about to become slightly polluted. We have a busy day ahead of us. Good night, Mr. Love, Mr. Piro, Miss Maruzzi—and Miss Cartier, wherever you are."

Madeleine didn't notice them leave.

"Nobody else can, Barclay. Nobody else can."

Sweet Harriet leaped out of bed and began pacing the floor in her bare feet, hands on hips, chin jutting out defiantly, face stippled with a pattern of dried tears and mascara. The traveling clock on the bureau said 4:28—three hours of tossing in bed, plotting and scheming, muted oaths and imprecations. Hate you, Madeleine. Hate you, Flora. Hate you, Fauna. Hate you, Sam Wyndham. Hate you, Zelma Wave and that fat blob of spawn from your womb.

"I'll be back on top again!" she screamed at the ceiling. "I don't care who I have to destroy to get there! I have nothing to fear but fear itself. As God is my witness, I'll never go hungry again. So fasten your seat belts, it's going to be a bumpy concert!"

The phone rang.

"Madeleine?" she shrieked into the mouthpiece.

"This is the desk," said the sleepy voice at the other end. "There's a complaint about some yelling in your room."

"Ahhhhhh, banana oil!" She slammed the phone down and resumed pacing the room, hands on hips, chin jutting out defiantly, scheming, plotting, scheming, plotting . . .

"Stay with me, Seth."

"Go to sleep, Madeleine. Swallow the aspirin and go to sleep."

"Stay with me. Please."

"Go to sleep, actress cat."

Madeleine struggled up and propped herself unsteadily on an elbow. "You here, too, mahogany cat? Goody goody gumdrops. We can have a three-way."

"Go to sleep, Madeleine." Seth eased her gently back onto the pillow.

"I'm afraid."

"There's nothing to be afraid of."

"Says you."

"Want me to sing you a lullaby, actress cat?"

"Do you know 'I'll Be Glad When You're Dead, You Rascal You'?"

"No, actress cat."

"Heh heh. Didn't think you did. Seth?"

"What, Madeleine?"

"I don't want to finish the book."

"You'll feel different tomorrow."

"No. I won't. I want to drop it. Then maybe Peter and Robert will drop it. Then everybody's safe . . . safe . . ."

"Safe from what?"

"Stay with me, Seth. I'm afraid. I don't want to be alone. I'm afraid. It's all gone too far. Too far. I knew it would someday. I knew it would."

And she was asleep. Seth motioned Pharoah to follow him to the door.

"May as well walk, cat. It's only five blocks or so."

"Cigarette?"

"Got one."

They walked in silence for a few moments, a silence finally disturbed by a stray cat knocking over a garbage-can cover.

"Cat," said Pharoah, "I think we are sitting on a time bomb."

"Peter and Robert don't frighten me."

"I noticed that at Ida's, baby cat. I'm proud of you. You didn't given an inch."

"I'm not afraid, Pharoah."

"I know that, baby. I said you wasn't, didn't I?"

"You don't understand me at all."

"Sure I do! Who understands you better than I do?"

"Peter and Robert."

Pharoah burst out laughing, just as Seth had predicted to himself he would.

"They know I murdered Ben Bentley."

Pharoah grabbed his shoulder and spun him around. They stood in the middle of the street staring at each other.

"They do, Pharoah," said Seth quietly. "You know they do. They haven't the proof, but they know. And very soon they're going to use it."

"I'll kill them."

"No you won't."

"I'll kill anybody who tries to hurt you."

"They're not afraid, Pharoah. They aren't writing the Barclay Mill story just to make a buck. It's a cover-up, and a good one. They laid their plan well. They want Barclay Mill's murderer. Don't you get it? Don't you see it? What they really want to know is—who they are."

8

"ROBERT," groaned Peter, head half hidden by his pillow, "does it really matter any more?"

"What are you alluding to?" asked Robert, sitting up in bed, a notebook propped against his knees, making an occasional entry with his ballpoint pen.

"Who we are. We're here. Isn't that enough?" Peter sat up and rested against the headboard.

"You had a bad night. You cried out twice and then wept very bitterly."

"I had a nightmare," said Peter, reaching for a cigarette from the nearly depleted pack on the night table. "We were burning Madeleine at the stake. And at her feet we laid the corpse of Seth Piro."

"But he *is* a corpse, isn't he? The walking dead. Embalmed and preserved by his possessive detective friend."

"I'm becoming rather fond of him."

"Pharoah Love?"

"Seth Piro."

"Yes, I rather sensed that when you tapped my shin under the table last night."

"You went too far."

"No farther than we agreed." A puff of smoke settled in a cloud over Robert's notebook.

"Much too far. He knows what we suspect and we've frightened him."

Robert dispersed the cloud with a wave of his hand. "He's far from frightened. He wins my admiration for that. Peter?"

"Yes, Robert."

"Mr. Piro is a very unhappy, very disillusioned, very

tired gentleman. I think if he had the courage he would destroy himself. But he doesn't and he won't. Instead he will plow his energies into solving the riddle of Barclay Mill's murder. He's our first lucky break. We must make the most of him. He's the liveliest by far of this aggregation of corpses we're dealing with. Our ladies died over three decades ago, but, like the vampires they are, they refuse to stay dead. Full marks for them, I suppose. But I for one cannot rest while I am incomplete. Order some breakfast. You'll feel better after you've eaten."

"We mustn't be his judges, Robert."

"Mr. Piro again?"

"His conscience is his cancer, Robert. It will take care of him in time."

"Peter," said Robert impatiently, "even if our deduction is correct, we are in no position to expose Mr. Piro's crime. It would be impossible to prove. We've read his book and we've seen the police file. The conclusions of both are flawless. I also happen to like Mr. Piro. I admire his composure in the face of adversity. There's so much of us in that. I admire the way he handles Madeleine. The kindness. The understanding. The empathy. Yes, there's a great deal of good in him. And the best is yet to come. He's going to lead us to Barclay Mill's murderer. And then we'll know who we are. Now order breakfast like a good little bunny while I inundate myself under the shower."

"Don't sing Wagner, Robert. It's not a good morning for Wagner. Room service, please."

"You awake, cat?"

"Awake."

Pharoah placed a cup of steaming black coffee on the night table and sat on the edge of Seth's bed.

"I'm going to put a little heat on our twin cats."

"No you're not." Seth sat up and reached for the coffee.

"Have to fight fire with fire, baby cat."

"There's nothing to worry about, Pharoah. Leave them alone."

"I'm trying to dig you, Seth cat, but my shovel's too

small." His words were like house detectives, sneaking down hallways, peeking in keyholes, tapping on doors that were reluctant to open.

"I've been up half the night thinking about it, Pharoah. And I think I'm right. Whether or not I murdered Ben isn't what's important to them. They want my help. Last night, in their own Gothic horror of a way, they were trying to let me know I can trust them. So lay off." Seth sipped the coffee while Pharoah looked at him, perplexed, attempting to X-ray his mind with the faulty machine he called his intuition. Seth reunited the cup and saucer, smiling impishly. Pharoah's face was as soberly frozen as Eric Sevareid's analyzing the Vietnam situation.

"You're a hell of a detective, Sherlock cat. Those boys didn't travel three thousand miles to pin a murder rap on me. I just happened to be here, like Mount Everest. They climbed to the top for practice and enjoyed the view. Now they're ready to scale the really *biiiig* mountain. And they have subtly invited me to join the party. Today I'm accepting the invitation."

Pharoah had lit a cigarette, but the unpleasant taste in his mouth wasn't due to the tobacco. "Cat, them boys are making a big wave, and somebody's going to get drowned."

"In times of disaster, kiddo, it's every man for himself. And let me tell you something, I feel very very stimulated by it all. I feel *reeeeally* good! I've got one of Ruthelma Kross's famous tingles." When Seth's literary agent felt good about anything, she tingled.

Seth leaped out of bed and began his setting-up exercises, inhaling and exhaling like a man who really believed he had healthy lungs.

"Cat—pay attention."

Seth snapped to attention and saluted.

"Which one of them dancing darlings killed Barclay Mill?"

"Don't know yet, Herr von Stroheim."

"Which one of them knows the truth about the twins?"

"Maybe all of them, Herr von Stroheim."

"Why won't they spill?"

"Fear, Herr von Stroheim."

"Stop the shit and pay attention!" snapped Pharoah.

Seth slumped into a chair, crossed his legs and folded his arms. "All I can figure out so far, Pharoah, is this. At least one of our ladies knows who killed Barclay Mill. One or more of them knows the twins' origins. I think Sam Wyndham knows something about something, too. Ditto Sweet Harriet. Enough for the two of them to remain on Madeleine's payroll for at least three decades. That could also mean Madeleine killed Barclay. But the Fleurs have provided her with a very strong alibi. Also, the way Barclay was murdered—shoved off a balcony and a broken neck—indicates it should have been a man who did it."

"Not necessarily, cat."

Seth nodded. "Right. A very, very furious woman can muster up an amazing amount of strength, especially if, due to a little booze, the victim is a little unsteady on his feet. The post-mortem on Barclay Mill showed he had been drinking a great deal. So who were the ladies who saw him that night? Flora. Fauna. Sweet Harriet found the body—she says. Zelma Wave was in San Francisco —and that could use a little checking. And Madeleine was waiting for the Fleurs when they got back from Barclay's, and he was presumably alive when they left him. And Sam Wyndham apparently never even figured in the investigation. Then there's the matter of those very hot love letters sent by the ladies to Barclay. And somehow they got into the hands of a newspaper that never revealed where it had got them and for how much. Letters from Flora, Fauna and Sweet Harriet. Madeleine hinted last night she knows the answer to that one."

"Whoever stole those letters and sold them couldn't be the murderer."

"Don't be so sure about that. It's a really beautiful way to avoid suspicion—or show the murderer they mean business. Such a lovely case! No wonder it keeps being rehashed and rehashed. But better yet, where do the Moulin twins figure? Madeleine says their mother and father were small-part players killed in an automobile crash. Be interesting to try and get their names and see if they ever appeared in any Barclay Mill spectacles. Be interesting to find out where and when the twins were born."

"I can put a tracer on it."

"Not yet."

"Why not?"

"Got the twins right here, Pharoah cat. I'll ask them myself."

"Fair enough. Now chew on this. You think murderer cat is just going to sit back and let you and the twin cats get too far?"

"That," said Seth, "is what's giving me my tingle. Murderer cat is going to have to make a move soon. And the only other person who knows that besides me and the twins is Madeleine Cartier."

"You like her a lot, Seth baby. Supposing she turns out to be your pigeon. She's been up on a murder rap before."

("But did the son of a bitch have to start beating me up in my kitchen and trip and fall on that bread knife I happened to be holding?")

"Where are you, cat? You're not reading me."

Seth was staring out the window, apparently deep in thought. "I'm way ahead of you. I was just wondering what really gave Madeleine her nervous breakdown after Barclay Mill was murdered. And now that I've met Sam Wyndham I just can't see Madeleine falling in love with him. I just can't see that at all." He snapped his fingers, crossed from the chair to the phone, flipped open his address book and dialed.

"Be gentle," cautioned Pharoah. "That'll be one whopper of a hangover she's nursing."

"My, my, my, Pharoah," and Seth clucked his tongue admonishingly, "you are certainly way off the beam this morning." Then into the phone, "Sam Wyndham? Seth Piro here. Not too early for you, I hope. In the mood for me today?"

Madeleine lay with her face buried in the pillow, her right arm and right leg hanging listlessly over the edge of the bed. The hundred singing athletes in her head were pounding a reprise of the "Anvil Chorus" and she knew only a triple Bromo-Seltzer would numb their arms and mute their voices. But she couldn't move.

What did I do last night? What did I say? Oh, go away, you noisy, sadistic sons of bitches, and let me think. There was Seth and there was Pharoah, and the boys and lots of champagne, and somebody danced on the table and sang "The Sorority Stomp" (how the hell did she remember the lyrics after all these years?) and probably made a big fat ass of herself. Who got me home? Who put me to bed? Did I get laid, with any luck?

She sat on the edge of the bed holding her head, wondering if she could make it to the bathroom and the Bromo-Seltzer. Oh, you wonderful Bromo-Seltzer. You've done so much in the past for Kathryn Murray and Ilka Chase in those television commercials. Can you do as much for me? With an effort, she got to her feet and staggered toward the bathroom.

Help! Who is this frightening apparition staring at me from the medicine-cabinet mirror? Who is this middle-aged horror with the crow's feet closing in around the bloodshot eyes, the ugly little creases bordering the once-seductive mouth, the tiny blotches of yellow on what were once fresh, brilliant apple-red cheeks. You are sad, frightening apparition. I shall cry for you.

Through her tears she opened the cabinet, found the Bromo, and poured four heaping capfuls into a glass, where tap water soon caused a white hurricane to appear. She drank the concoction in three gulps and then sat down on the john, still holding the glass and staring at the white-tiled floor. The sonorous belch was more melodic to her than the "Anvil Chorus." The sigh that followed it was more of despair than relief. She struggled to her feet again, placed the glass back in its niche, and gently wended her way back to the bedroom.

She lit a cigarette with unsteady hands and momentarily entertained the notion of setting fire to the bed, but the match had flickered out and she flung it on the floor, leaving a slight wisp of smoke, a slight odor of sulphur and a slight but not too pressing desire to return to the bathroom and throw up.

She drew the ostrich-feather negligee around her shoulders, walked unsteadily to the living room, and sat in the chair by the window that afforded the beautiful view of Central Park.

Christ. Tonight. Concert. Peter. Robert. Seth. Memoirs. Television series. Sweet Harriet. Comeback. Flora. Fauna. Sixteen-millimeter projectors. Sam. Memwahs. Zelma. Death. Destruction. Barclay. Scandal. Somebody put a hand in my head and pull out the winning number.

"I've got to do something," she said to the window, "I've got to do something. Heavy, heavy hangs over my head. Hangs over lots of heads."

She shivered and drew the negligee tighter.

I can't run away. There's no place to run to. I can't walk out on the series. I can't walk out on the book. I can't run away from murder.

Murder.

Maybe I'm wrong. Maybe it'll fade away like an old general. But it won't. I looked into that face and I saw murder, and I can't do anything about it. I can't. I can't.

The shame of it all.

Flora held the telephone in a bone-crushing grip. The spoon in Fauna's right hand was frozen in mid-air, tiny globules of farina spilling over and dropping back into the bowl directly beneath.

"Madeleine!" boomed Flora. "You'll do no such thing!"

"My mind's made up," said Madeleine evenly, making a moué into the hand mirror. " 'Tis a far, far better thing and all that crap. Tonight's concert marks my farewell appearance. I'm folding my tent and stealing away. The first and only unselfish gesture of my life."

"You've got to make this comeback for us, baby," Flora pleaded. "It's all we've been living for."

"It's not worth the price."

"No matter what you do, you'll still have to shell out!"

"That's not what I'm talking about. Canceling out the book and the series—"

"Won't cancel out anything else!" Flora interjected sharply.

Fauna placed the spoon in the bowl and reached for the deck of cards.

"It had better, Flora," said Madeleine firmly, "it had just better. Seth Piro and the twins are on the verge of coming up with a couple of answers I want left unanswered. And this is the only way I know how to stop them."

"There are other ways," countered Flora quietly.

"No there aren't!" shouted Madeleine.

"Okay, baby," said Flora, "whatever you say. But what becomes of you? A lonely old lady in a lonely old house for the rest of your life? Reproaching yourself for throwing aside what might have been?"

"I won't be so lonely," said Madeleine, somewhat airily. "I just might adopt a little boy—say one of about twenty-five or -six."

"Madeleine!" snapped Flora. "I won't let you do this to yourself!"

"You should have thought of that thirty-three years ago."

"What the hell did you *think* I was thinking about then?"

"Flora," cautioned Fauna as she spread the cards on the table, "the neighbors."

"Fuck 'em!" snapped Flora, then back into the phone, "Madeleine? Now hear this. You're staying right here in New York and doing the series and finishing the book. Don't interrupt! It's *your* fault all our lives got messed up. You hear me?"

"I hear you." Weakly. Dull. Flat. Beaten.

"Well, keep listening, because I'm not finished. Anything you do now is an empty gesture, because it's too goddam late. The chips are down. You're going to see this thing through because *I'm* going to see to it that you do. You hear me?"

"I hear you."

"O.K. See you at the concert." Bang went the phone. "Flora."

"WHAT?"

Fauna burst into tears. Flora crossed to her and enveloped Fauna in her massive arms. "Don't cry, baby. I'm sorry. Honest to God, I'm sorry."

"It's the cards," Fauna wailed, "the cards! Look. Just look! Nothing but spades. Death! Death! We're surrounded by death!"

I can't do anything about it, Madeleine repeated to herself. I can't, I can't, I can't.

But on the other hand . . .

On the narrow window of the tiny shop on MacDougal Street in the heart of Greenwich Village was neatly lettered:

MANDALAY
Francis K. Mill, Prop.

Because of the name "Mandalay," tourists frequently blundered into the store under the impression it was a Chinese restaurant. Francis K. went to great pains to explain to them that Mandalay was the name of a motion picture that starred Kay Francis in 1934 and was produced by the Warner Brothers and that he was sort of named after Kay Francis which is why he selected the title of his mother's favorite Kay Francis movie as a name for his establishment which sold old movie magazines, posters, stills and other cinema artifacts and would they like to look around as browsing was permitted, and the tourists would marvel at how he could explain all this in one extremely foul-smelling breath.

Francis K. nervously held the phone, patiently waiting for acknowledgment from the other end, when Countess Vronsky entered with Lad, A Dog.

Said Countess Vronsky imperiously, "We have come to look at stills of Adele Mara and Acquanetta."

"And maybe Armida," Lad, A Dog chimed in, "if our heads aren't spinning by then."

Francis K. pointed to the shelves at the rear of the store, then spoke in a rush into the phone. "Oh, Miss Cawtier, yaw line's been so busy! This is Fwancis K. Mill. I got your numbuh fwom Celebwity Suhvice. Mummy wants to see you. She says it's uhgent. Could you please? I'd be evuh so gwateful! We live in Gwennitch Village on MacDougal Stweet, just above my tiny empowium . . ."

Madeleine wrote down the address, said goodbye, hung up, and then re-examined her make-up job in the hand mirror. Not too bad.

Then: Zelma Wave after all these years. She says it's "uhgent."

She's fwightened.

So am I, baby. So am I.

Sam Wyndham's garden apartment on East Fifty-fifth Street was neater and tidier than Sam, Seth observed.

"Martini O.K.?" asked Sam, pressing the ice bag to his temple, at which it frequently worshiped.

"Just fine, Sam. Have you tried aspirin?"

"Built up an immunity to them," sighed Sam. "The hell with it. I've got cirrhosis, you know."

"I didn't."

"Thought maybe Madeleine might've told you. According to my doctor, I should have been dead six months ago." Sam mustered a chuckle. "We Wyndhams don't die easy. Well. Out with it. What do you think I can do for you? Am I supposed to sing into that thing?" He indicated Seth's miniature tape recorder, which rested on the coffee table between them. "Christ, my head's killing me."

"What was Barclay Mill like?"

"A tired Greek god, if it's his looks you're referring to. He was in his early forties when he got bumped, you know. Suave, sophisticated, still built like a brick crap house. There wasn't a kid in his chorus lines who wouldn't go down on her knees for him. And I don't mean begging for mercy, either. Not at first, anyway."

"You worked on all his pictures."

"All of them."

"Easy to get along with?"

"Not bad."

"Any enemies?"

"No one outstanding, if that's what you're getting at. At least not to the naked eye."

"Who do you think killed him?"

"No idea."

(Too quick, thought Seth. He was ready for that one.)

"How sick was Madeleine when she came to Mexico?"

"Almost catatonic."

"That bad."

Sam ached for a martini of his own, but decided it was best to wait until after Seth left.

"And romance snapped her out of it?" he heard Seth ask.

"Gradually."

"No doctor?"

"There was one for a while. Some German refugee. Probably one of the first to get out, now that I think of it. There were about a handful of refugees in Cuernavaca at the time waiting for entry permits into the States."

"Remember his name?"

"Hell, no. Probably dead by now—or else he's over a hundred."

"You and Madeleine never had children, did you?"

"No, kid. Never wanted any."

"Was Madeleine in love with you when she married you?"

"Why else would she have married me?"

Seth had taken a sip of his martini, and it was Sam's first vicarious thrill of the day.

"Out of gratitude perhaps," suggested Seth in response to Sam's question. "You did promise to help re-establish her in Hollywood, didn't you?"

"That wasn't so hard. Mill's murder barely touched her, and by the time we got back it was yesterday's news. Besides, the *Follies of '32*, was in release and the trade papers had commented on Madeleine's potentials. Madeleine knew how to use her potentials."

"Where do the Moulin twins figure?"

Sam's eyes narrowed. "What do you mean?"

"Madeleine overdotes on them."

"Why shouldn't she? She discovered them, didn't she? She's their 'Auntie Madeleine.' Invested their money for them. Saw them through high school and college. Took a show into Korea just in hopes of seeing them. That's how Madeleine is when she loves anyone. All or nothing."

"All or nothing." Seth took another sip of his martini, and Sam squirmed in his seat. "Didn't she have an affair with Barclay Mill?"

"She told me he made a pass at her, but he didn't score."

("Ida, woman to woman, do you think I'm a nymphomaniac?")

"What about Fauna and Sweet Harriet?"

"What about them?"

"How'd they get along during the shooting of *Follies of '32?*"

"Peaches and cream."

"Even though Mill had thrown over Sweet Harriet for Fauna?"

"He'd have thrown over Fauna for somebody else had he lived."

"But Fauna said she and Mill were going to be married."

"That's what Fauna said. We'll never know Barclay's side of that story, will we?"

"Sam," said Seth steadily, toying with the stem of the martini glass, "isn't it unusual in a divorce for the wife to pay the husband alimony?"

Sam lowered the ice bag, and for a nervous moment Seth thought he was going to wind up and pitch.

"Madeleine's told me you're on her payroll."

"She helps me out every so often." *Why is your voice shaking, Sam?* "As you can see, we're still good friends."

"Is that why Sweet Harriet's on her payroll?"

"I don't know anything about that!" *I know this—I*

need a drink and I wish to hell you'd get out of here. "What the hell is this, anyway? You writing a book or conducting an investigation?"

"They go together," smiled Seth, "like Sodom and Gomorrah."

"I'll bet Madeleine doesn't know the kind of questions you're asking," said Sam in a childishly petulant voice.

"Sweet of Sweet Harriet to donate those new projectors."

Sam jumped to his feet. "Interview's over. Beat it. We've had it."

"O.K., Sam," sighed Seth, "O.K." He switched off the tape recorder and placed it in his pocket. "See you at the concert tonight?"

"See you in hell"—flinging the door open, Sam's trembling hand causing the knob to rattle.

You probably will, thought Seth as the door slammed shut behind him.

Sam gulped the remainder of Seth's drink, and the phone rang. Hand still trembling, he lifted it to his ear. "Hello."

"You said we had to talk, big boy. What's on your mind?"

"Murder," said Sam. "Murder's on my mind."

9

MADELEINE WAS buffeted by the waves of shock that engulfed her. "You're looking well, Zelma," she lied.

"Barclay would have called for a retake on that line, Madeleine."

Madeleine flicked her ash and mustered a smile. "Sorry. I was thinking, 'There but for the grace of God . . .'"

"There but for the grace of Barclay, you mean. If you'd like a drink or some coffee, you'll have to help yourself. When I need something," Zelma indicated the cane that lay across her lap, "I bang on the floor and Francis K. comes running. In case you're wondering, I didn't get you here to tap your till. I wanted you to know that the nonsense of my writing my memoirs is just that— nonsense. Francis K. is very impressionable, and Sam knows how to make an impression."

"You've nothing to be frightened about," said Madeleine evenly.

"I've *plenty* to be frightened about! Francis K. spotted a few reactions when he pulled ᵗʰe memoirs bit last night. There are a few people who still think I know more about Barclay's murder than I've admitted. Well, I don't. You tell them that. I don't!" The gnarled fingers touched the cane—perhaps, thought Madeleine, to ward off an invisible enemy. "They should let sleeping dogs lie, that's what they should do—let sleeping dogs lie. The twins told Francis K. they want to see me. I don't want to see them. I want Francis K. and me to be left alone!"

"You should have thought of that before letting Francis K. make his appearance last night."

Zelma groaned, attempting to shackle Madeleine to her

despair. "He didn't tell me he was to be a—" with an ironic smile—"guest of honor. He didn't tell me you or the other girls would be there. And Francis K. never has many moments of glory." Sadly, "You've seen him. You could tell for yourself. His world is limited to me, this apartment, and his shop." Proudly, "And he's built a fine business down there. He knows more about old movies than anybody! But he's *anonymous.*" She searched Madeleine's face. She saw compassion there and was proud she could still cause an effect. "He's very unhappy now. He's always prayed for a few days in the sun. My memoirs might have done that for him. And he's too innocent to understand the danger."

"Now, Zelma darling," joshed Madeleine, "what danger?"

"Murder, Madeleine, murder." Her voice faded into a ghostly whisper, and Madeleine shivered and sought warmth from a drag on her cigarette. "Somebody might just be thinking I've known all along who murdered Barclay." Madeleine started to remonstrate, but Zelma was too quick for her. "Don't tell me I'm crazy. I know all of you. Don't forget that. I know all of you well. Ambitious. Selfish. Determined!" Zelma's roll call made Madeleine uneasy. It annoyed her when people called their shots accurately. "I used to marvel at how you kids stopped at nothing to get what you wanted. I really did. Oh, why the hell didn't I quit when I was ahead? Why'd I think he'd ever come back to me?"

She burst into tears and Madeleine was stumped for a proper reaction. She ground the cigarette into an ashtray and cleared her throat.

"Now, Zelma," she began authoritatively, "you're making a mountain out of a molehill. Nobody's going to harm you or your son."

Zelma lifted her head slowly and stared at Madeleine. "Are you so sure?"

"Positive."

"What about the twins?"

"What about them?"

"Francis K. got the feeling they won't stop till they find Barclay's murderer."

"The murderer's probably dead!" snapped Madeleine.

"I don't think so," said Zelma softly, "and neither do you. You know more about it than you've ever let on, don't you, Madeleine? So do the others. And Sam. What's Sam after? Who's he trying to frighten? Why else did he use Francis K. last night?"

"Sam's sick. He's dying. He's a fool. He was always a fool. I'll take care of Sam."

"What's he after?" Zelma repeated.

Madeleine sighed. "The same thing I'm after. The same thing Sweet Harriet's after. The same thing Francis K. wants. Another moment in the sun. Sam always wanted to be a director. He wants to direct my first TV script. But he won't, because he's no good at it and he never was. He's trying to force me to demand that my producer use him. I can't be forced any more. Because I don't care what happens from now on."

"I don't believe you."

"It's true, Zelma. It's true." She shook her head sadly. "I've tried to run away, but I can't. I'm stuck. Trapped. I'm in a wheelchair of another sort. It's all gone too far. Just because I didn't stop to think." She paused for a moment. "I didn't stop to think! Isn't that one hell of an epitaph?"

She stood up, crossed to the invalid and put her hand on her cheek affectionately. "Can't anything be done for you?"

"Don't let them come after me and the boy."

"I mean *this*. The wheel chair."

"I'm all right. I'm used to it." Zelma moved her head and kissed the tips of Madeleine's fingers. "Forgive me, Madeleine. If I had it, I'd give back every cent I took from you."

"I wouldn't know what to do with it," said Madeleine sharply. "Goodbye, Zelma. And stop fretting. You and your son are perfectly safe. If you need anything, phone me." At the doorway she turned and asked, "Don't you ever get out of this apartment?"

"Not too often."

"I was just wondering. There's an open-air concert in Central Park tonight. A musical tribute to Barclay Mill. It's too bad you have to miss it—though I bet there'll be a few sour notes."

Sweet Harriet's iron-gray eyes were bemused as she watched Sam Wyndham's trembling hand lift the martini glass to his lips. She was grating a fingernail with an emery board.

Sam winced. "Can't you cut that out?"

"Say, Krazy Kat"—her voice out-grating the emery board—"you better put a string around your bundle of nerves. Nobody's got *me* worried. This kid knows how to look after Number One!" She jabbed her chest with her newly emeried thumb. "And all the rest is banana oil! Madeleine's gonna give us exactly what we want, because she can't afford no more scandals. *You*"—jabbing an index finger in his direction—"are gonna direct that first script, and *this* baby"—fingers reversed and thumb jabbing the chest—"is gonna play Madeleine's kid sister. She ain't giving us the brush *that* easy. Or else"—her voice grinding into gear—"I spill a few memoirs of my own. Put that in your pipe, kiddo."

"Ah, stop kidding yourself," said Sam wearily, "neither one of us has a hope in hell. We're finished."

"I am *not finished!*" screeched Sweet Harriet, leaping to her feet and stabbing the air in front of Sam's face with the emery board. "This kid should be riding in limousines instead of taxis!"

"Grow up, for crying out loud!" shouted Sam. "You're a middle-aged woman. Madeleine told you to stay put in Hollywood, and you should have stayed put. You fouled up the works the minute you started tippy-tap-toeing up Broadway!"

"Horse feathers!" She sneered the two words so beautifully, it was almost poetic. "You wanna see the fan mail I got after I did that interview show? My public wants me back. What I'm giving 'em now is a new image. You ain't backing out on me, you hear me? You ain't backing out on me! This director Madeleine's got now don't want me. And I'll see to it she gets rid of him and puts you in his place. And then *you'll* see to it"—another stab into space with the emery board—"that I get to play that kid sister."

She broke into a thirty-second time step for emphasis.

"Stop that, dammit! Stop it!" he shouted. "It's embarrassing!"

Hands on hips, chin jutting out, iron-gray eyes narrowed into meaningful slits, tiny Sweet Harriet seemed to tower over the wreck of the man slumped in the easy chair, lifting the martini glass to his mouth with both hands.

"You pipsqueak." Her hand shot out and knocked the glass from his hand. "I oughtta brain you. Two mistakes I made in my life, and you're the second. Well, you're one mistake I can correct."

"You won't live that long."

"Says you!"

"Why can't you be satisfied with that hundred bucks a week she gives you?"

"Money," sneered Sweet Harriet, drawing herself up haughtily, "ain't everything. It is my artistry that counts!"

"Even if there hadn't been a scandal when Barclay was murdered, you wouldn't have lasted another year in pictures. You were on your way out and you know it. That's why you stole those damn love letters and sold them to the newspaper. You thought *then* you'd be giving yourself a new image. Give your career a new shot in the arm. You should have gotten a shot in the head."

"So she told you about that, did she?"

"Yeah, she told me about that."

Sweet Harriet made a swipe at her purse and connected. "I'll fix her for that. Now I'll really fix her for that! You going to that concert tonight?" Sam shook his head. "Well, change your mind, big boy. You be there.

I'm gonna make that concert something none of you will ever forget. So long, big boy–and thanks for the buggy ride, if you catch my drift!"

She clickety-clacked to the door, pulled it open, did another thirty-second time step, and pulled the door shut behind her.

An excruciating pain shot through Sam's abdomen, and he doubled over, clutching his stomach, eyes misting with tears, face contorted in agony. Take me, God, take me, he prayed. Dear Jesus, take me. Dear Jesus, get me out of here. Take me before I get sent.

"Flora."

"Not now, Fauna," growled Flora, "I'm thinking."

"I was just wondering. Will God forgive us?"

"Well," sighed Flora, "he's been playing along with us up to now. We must be doing something right."

"Do you know something?" said Fauna, clasping her hands together and smiling wispily, "I feel better now than I've felt in months."

"Do you baby? Flora's glad. I wish a little of it would spread to me."

"Don't be afraid, Flora. Everything will turn out all right in the end."

"One thing's got me worried, Fauna."

"What's that, Flora?"

"Madeleine. I keep worrying she just might crack up again."

"I hope not, Flora. I do sincerely hope not."

I'll fix them. I'll fix them flappers real good.

Only one or two people she passed felt genuinely sorry for the crazy lady talking to herself as she clickety-clacked along the street. Sweet Harriet always used gestures when she talked to herself, and when her brain was blazing with anger, bursting with a plan for revenge, the gestures were sharper and ominously violent. She would sometimes stop and stamp her foot to emphasize a particularly gnawing inner fury. Occasionally anger gave way to self-pity, and then her lower lip would tremble and she would whimper. Twice dogs barked at her and frightened mistresses pulled at their leashes, signaling them to mind their own business.

"I told you to wait till I sent for you." Madeleine's angry words were piercing her thoughts. "But no, not our dear Sweet Harriet. Always has to jump the gun. Always has to move in and screw everything up even before it gets going. Well, there's no place in the series for you and that's that. They don't want you and I'm tired of fighting. You've made a laughingstock of yourself with those stupid exhibitions. And don't start threatening me. Destroy me and you destroy yourself."

"Why couldn't you wait?" It was Flora booming now. "Madeleine told you to wait wait wait until she sees how the series turns out. She can't make demands now. She can be replaced. Once the show's a success, then it's a different story. But you couldn't wait till she secured her position. You had to come here now and carry on in the streets like a candidate for the booby-hatch. Don't you threaten me, you little stinker! I ain't afraid of you! Just remember, our funerals mean your funeral, too. Now get off Madeleine's back or else . . ."

Barclay? Is that you, Barclay?

"Little dear one," he purred as he patted her cheek, "did you have to stir up such a fuss with the front office? Don't you know they only renew options when I advise them to? They can only use you in musicals. You can't act. They took the gamble once and let you play Camille. Camille lost and so did the studio. Ten tins of film languishing on the shelf. My dear, if they ever released it to the theaters you'd be laughed off the screen. Now, don't try to cross me again, dear one. Madeleine Cartier has a very promising career ahead of her. Very foolish of you to try to have her cut out of the movie. Only I have the power to do that. Yes, little dear one, the picture is much too long. And I just might omit your big 'Tippy-Tap-Toe' number. Now, now, now. No tears. No tantrums. I said I just might, I didn't say I would. You're so self-destructive, little dear one. So terribly self-destructive. And carrying tales to Fauna and Flora isn't very wise, either. Not very wise at all."

"I'm smarter than all of you!" she screeched, stamping her foot on the sidewalk. "You'll see! You'll see! I'll fix you! I'll fix all of you! If I don't make it, then none of you will!"

"Mommy, Mommy, Mommy!" wept the little boy running into the apartment house, "there's a crazy lady on the street!"

"Charming apartment, Mr. Piro, absolutely charming apartment. And you've laid out coffee and cookies. How thoughtful. Peter, come look at this view. Is that one of the *Queens* I see, Mr. Piro?"

Seth glanced out the window. "The *Mary*."

"How proud she looks."

"If you'd rather have a drink," offered Seth, "I'm well stocked."

"No, thank you," said Peter.

"Coffee's fine," said Robert.

Seth sat and filled three cups with steaming black liquid. Peter and Robert sat opposite him on the couch. By invisible signal, they crossed their legs simultaneously, then spooned two teaspoonfuls of sugar into their cups and stirred. Seth wondered if he ought to applaud.

"You didn't sound too surprised when we phoned," said Robert.

"I knew you would." Seth sipped his coffee and it was almost as strong as his self-assurance. When he looked up, the twins were smiling as they contemplated him.

"Peter thought I went too far last night."

"In which direction?"

"Ben Bentley's murder."

Seth shrugged. "I didn't think you went too far at all. Your analysis was extremely astute."

"Thank you," said Robert. "Then I gather we understand each other completely."

"Appreciate," suggested Seth, "as much as understand. And we can be of use to each other, can't we?"

Robert spoke. "What did I tell you, Peter? I knew we'd found a comrade-in-arms in Mr. Piro."

"Seth," said Seth.

"Seth. So Biblical. So charming." Robert uncrossed his legs and leaned forward. "Let's get down to business, Seth. Our mission in New York is twofold. We wish to uncover our identity and Barclay Mill's murderer. We're positive we can't pinpoint one without the other. At least one or more of five people can give us the answers we seek—Madeleine, Flora Fleur, Fauna, Sam Wyndham and Sweet Harriet. What has Madeleine told you about us?"

"Other than getting you out of the orphanage into the Screen Actors' Guild? That your mother and father were small-part players killed in an automobile crash."

"A canard," sniffed Peter. "The actors in question were killed *prior* to our birth. Someone was very careless about choosing *them* as our mythical progenitors. Secondly—if I may continue, Robert?"

"Carry on."

"We cannot find a trace of any record of our birth. We were admitted to the orphanage in June of 1933, at the age of four months."

"By whom?" asked Seth, munching a Hydrox.

"By a woman named Matilda Myelnitsa," said Robert.

"Who's Matilda Myelnitsa?"

Peter sighed. "A beautiful question, Seth. We haven't the vaguest idea. And no one at the orphanage today can help us. The lady who made the arrangements with the mysterious Matilda has long since crossed the great divide and we strongly suspect her palm had been crossed with silver in return for her silence. We assume we were born sometime in March of 'thirty-three approximately six months after Barclay Mill's murder. We were the darlings of the orphanage, of course, because we were absolutely adorable. We also learned that large sums of money were contributed anonymously to the institution in our names. So naturally particular care was taken in our upbringing, and our every whim was catered to. We had a large variety of whims."

"We were spoiled rotten," interjected Robert.

"Don't editorialize, Robert. In 1946 there was a talent search for twins to appear in a Madeleine Cartier movie, and you know the rest. She's been like a mother to us ever since. In fact, for a brief period she spent a great deal of money on private detectives in an attempt to help re-create our beginning; that's when she came up with the two killed in the automobile crash. Robert and I later investigated them thoroughly. They had come to this country as understudies with a troupe of Russian actors and stayed on when the troupe returned to Russia. Made their way to Hollywood and found work in silent pictures. Talkies finished them, except for an occasional role for him as waiter or butler and for her as waitress or maid. It was impossible to trace their relatives. This Myelnitsa might have been a friend. Of course we've suspected from the start Madeleine knows who we really are. She steadfastly denies this."

"I might get better results with her." Seth refilled their cups.

"That's what we were hoping you'd say," beamed Peter.

"What I don't understand," said Seth, "is why, if your mother and possibly father are still alive, either one has been reluctant to step forward. Especially when you were starring in pictures."

"Excellent observation." Robert clapped his hands gently in approval. "Fear is what kept them silent. Fear because somewhere in the past one or the other was involved in a scandal, a scandal that in some way might erupt again if they dared reassociate themselves with us. The only scandal that occurred at the time of our birth was the Barclay Mill affair. And as you well know, the five surviving protagonists of that little mess live in fear of the murderer being unveiled. Which brings us back to the beginning. One or more of those five people can give us the answers we seek."

"We're positive of this," said Peter, "because our presence in New York has unnerved them all. They thought we'd stay safely tucked away in our precious cottage at

Malibu Beach writing our true crime stories. Little did they realize the crime-story ploy was the foundation we cleverly laid to bring us eventually to tackling the Barclay Mill case."

"Now, then, Seth"—a whirlpool eddying in Robert's cup as he stirred it vigorously—"this brings us to the murderer. Who's your most likely candidate?"

"The most obvious one is Sweet Harriet."

"Why?"

"She says she found the body. She says Mill was dead when she got there. There was no one to corroborate her statement. And yet the police apparently took her word for it."

"Right!" cried Peter. "But only because the studio pulled strings and paid an enormous sum to kill the entire investigation. The studios, as you well know, do that frequently. Have you a second candidate waiting in the wings?"

"Madeleine."

"Interesting," said Robert, "very interesting. Why Madeleine?"

"From something Sam Wyndham said this morning."

"Ah!" cried Peter. "The Wyndham interview!"

"Sam told me that when Madeleine was brought to Cuernavaca by Flora and Fauna she was, as he put it, 'almost catatonic.' It takes one hell of a shock to put someone in that kind of state. The way Madeleine tells it, it was because the studio dropped her option on account of her association with Flora, Fauna and Sweet Harriet. That sounded very weak when she said it. If she was in the clear as far as the scandal was concerned, why drop her option at all? There had to be more to it than that. And I intend to work on it."

Robert began ticking the names off on his fingers. "Number one, Sweet Harriet, the saccharine horror who is capable of anything, including murder. Number two, Madeleine, whom we adore and revere, but murder is murder. Which leaves . . ."

"Flora, Fauna and Sam Wyndham," reeled off Peter.

"And Zelma Wave," added Seth softly.

"Zelma Wave?" Robert looked at Peter, who shrugged. "But she was in San Francisco at the time."

"Pharoah's trying to check that for me. It won't be easy, but he's trying."

"Ah!" Peter smiled. "So glad he's trying to be of assistance. Let's hope he's a better detective on this than he was on the Bentley—" Peter's leg connected with Robert's shin again.

Seth lit a cigarette. "I have a date with Sweet Harriet at three."

"And we have one at four," said Robert, rubbing his shin. "Shall we meet again at five and compare notes?"

"Let's meet at Ida's," suggested Seth. "I won't have much time. Pharoah and I are escorting Madeleine to tonight's concert."

"Ah, yes. The concert, Peter. We mustn't miss that."

"We don't miss much, do we, Robert?"

As Seth was about to open the door, Robert stayed his hand. "I'm sure there's no need to caution you."

"About what?"

"Our delightfully unholy alliance. Our suspects must never be apprised we are working in tandem."

Peter's face widened into a wall-to-wall grin. "Perhaps a password and a secret handshake are in order."

"Perhaps you'd like a swift kick in the pants?" offered Robert. Then, patting Seth's shoulder, "You realize, of course, our investigation has probably aroused the sleeping tiger in Barclay Mill's assassin. The three of us—" pausing for a beautifully theatrical emphasis—"might be marked for murder. Therefore I prescribe a few ounces of caution. Till later."

Alone, a few moments later, Seth sat by the window watching a helicopter hovering over the traffic on the West Side Highway. What was that Madeleine said last night? "Heavy, heavy hangs over my head."

"And mine," sighed Seth, "and mine."

10

"IT'S A SKULL, I tell you! It is! It is!"

Flora leaned over and peered into Fauna's teacup. The residue of soggy tea leaves lay there complacently, defying analysis. Flora hmm'd and then screwed up her face. "I don't see it."

Madeleine lunged out of her chair, grabbed the teacup and smashed it against the wall. Fauna shrieked and Flora slammed her beefy fist on the table.

"Curb that temper, girl! Take a pill, Fauna. Sit down, Madeleine, you're wearing out the carpet."

"Trapped!" shouted Madeleine. "I'm trapped!"

"She's getting hysterical," whimpered Fauna, "she's cracking up! Like she did then!"

"There's nothing left in me to crack up!" shouted Madeleine. "It was all ground to dust years ago!" She shifted gears magnificently. "I've got a marvelous idea. Why don't the three of us go on a cruise to the West Indies? The series doesn't start shooting for another month yet, and by the time we get back Peter and Robert will have left town and Seth Piro will have quit the book in disgust."

"Balls." Flora was sweeping up the pieces of broken crockery, the cigarette dangling from her lips and jiggling like a semaphore as she spoke. "What about Harriet? What about Sam? No, sweetheart"—crossing to the kitchen—"the orchestra's all tuned up and we've got to face the music."

"Flora—Flora, I'm begging you." Madeleine's arms were outstretched like a Red Cross nurse on a recruiting poster. She heard the broken crockery crash into the garbage pail, the exclamation point to an unspoken refusal.

"O.K., then!" snapped Madeleine, grabbing her purse. "Do whatever the hell you like. I'm out of it. Do you hear me, Flora? I'm out of it!"

Flora loomed large in the doorway, wiping her hands on the dish towel.

"Madeleine."

As though an electrical shock had charged through her fingers, Madeleine pulled her hand away from the door-knob.

"Nobody's going to find out nothing," stated Flora flatly, "and that's *that*. That agreement we made thirty-three years ago *holds* and you're *sticking* to it. Peter and Robert don't frighten me, because if they ever get to the truth they won't dare share it with anyone else. As for the Piro creep, he's still walking around in circles and that's what he'll be doing for the rest of his life. Do I have to remind you what you owe *us*?"

"No."

"Then go on home and get some rest, pretty one." She crossed to Madeleine and embraced her tightly. "I want you to knock them cold at that concert tonight. I want you back on top again—where we belong. It's all we've lived for. It's all we've got. We can't face ending our lives in this stinking hole." Her voice broke.

"All right darling," whispered Madeleine, "all right. I'll go along with the tide." She patted Flora's cheek. "I'll phone you later."

It's not the heat, thought Madeleine, its the humidity, as she walked with a slow, measured pace to her hotel. That's why my skin is so damp and my hands feel so clammy. It's not fear, it's humidity. Maybe I'm wrong. Maybe nothing will happen. Maybe it'll all blow over the way darling Jerry Giesler used to say it would every time he led me into court. Zelma Wave doesn't know a thing, and neither Sweet Harriet nor Sam dares spill a word of what they know. Flora's probably right. She usually is. Didn't she know better than any of us how to handle Barclay? It would have been clear sailing if I hadn't been such an idiot. ("Do I have to remind you what you owe *us?*") Everything, Flora. Everything. But what about Peter, what about Robert, what about poor, sweet Seth? Oh, dear God. What's the answer? I haven't one. Not yet. Not now. I can't think straight. Oh, the hell with it. In the words of another great slut: Fiddle-dee-dee, I'll worry about it tomorrow.

"Don't push me, big boy. Sweet Harriet takes her own sweet time about everything."

Sly little vixen, thought Seth, staring at the smiling creature seated next to him on the couch, nibbling a carrot stick. Pointed little vixen teeth, sharp little vixen nose, shrewd little vixen eyes. What an elusive quarry you'd be in a foxhunt. Here's one hound who can testify to that.

"There's no rush," said Seth. "I just thought it was rather strange you never got to meet the Moulin twins, considering how close you've always been to Madeleine."

"There's close, kiddo"—voice twanging like a plucked banjo string—"and there's close. I didn't see too much of Madeleine because we agreed a long time ago it would be better that way." The iron-gray vixen eyes were fixed on the ceiling. "But we kept in touch all right. We sure kept in touch."

Flattery. That might be the ticket. It worked yesterday in the bank. One flattery coming up.

"I'm surprised you haven't been snapped up for a Broadway show."

Her eyes traveled from the ceiling to Seth's face, carefully searching for a trace of mockery.

"I think you could wrap up this town and wear it like a trophy."

She threw back her head and laughed, a steady outpour of piccololike hee-hee-hee-hee-hees. "Don't you think I've had some offers? But I won't audition! Legendary figures like me shouldn't have to audition. What do them amateurs know? That Alexander something and that Leland whateverthehellhisname is. Me?" She was on her feet jabbing her thumb at her meager chest. "Me audition? When you're immortal, you don't have to prove yourself any more. They should be writing shows *espe-*

cially for *me*. Sayyyyy!" She snapped her fingers and did the thirty-second-time step. "Why don't *you* write me a show?"

Seth paled as she bounced back onto the couch next to him and threw her arms around his neck.

"Come on, big feller, write this kid a show. What do you say, big boy?"

"It's a thought," he managed to say. "I just might give it some thought, at that."

"You're jazzing me." She drew away from him, fingering the small string of pearls around her neck.

"No I'm not"—hoping he sounded sincere. "Of course, I've never written a show before, but it might be fun to try."

"Nah! Save that booshwah for Madeleine." She was on her feet, hands on hips, pacing the floor with that unique, tough-kid little walk of hers. "You're soft-soaping me. What's with you and the twins?" She had planted herself in front of him, tapping one foot impatiently. "Come on, big boy. Out with it. You in cahoots with them?"

"I'm in cahoots with no one. I'm only trying to do my job. Gather material for Madeleine's memoirs."

"Sure you are." The sneer in her voice clawed at his ears. "You gonna be at that concert tonight?"

"I wouldn't miss it for the world."

"O.K., big boy. 'Cause so's this kid. And that's gonna make it a memorable evening!"

"Have they asked you to perform?" Trying to sound pleased, but puzzled.

"Nobody's asked me nothing. I'm gonna give them something for free! And that's all I'm gonna tell you. They think they can push me out of the picture just like that." She snapped her fingers an inch from Seth's nose. "Well, I'll show them. Memorial for Barclay Mill. I'll give them something to remember all right. Now there's the door. You and me—we've had it."

Seth didn't budge.

"I said we had it!" she screeched. "Now twenty-three skiddoo!"

Seth rose and pocketed the tape recorder. "Sweet Harriet," he said with slow deliberation, "you are a very foolish immortal."

"Says you! If I don't make it, then nobody else is gonna make it! This kid's got guts she ain't used yet. I'm not afraid of nothing. And let me tell you this, butter-and-egg man"—flouncing to the door and flinging it open—"I'm gonna rock this town like it's never been rocked before. And you can tell that to Madeleine and Flora and Fauna and all the rest of your gang. Now *out!*" With an amazing show of strength, she shoved Seth into the hallway and slammed the door shut.

Legendary figure, thought Seth, that was an amazing show of strength. A very amazing show of strength.

Sweet Harriet screeched into the phone. "Desk? Miss Dimple! I ain't in to anybody no more, you hear me? There's a set of twins due here in fifteen minutes. Well, you tell them Sweet Harriet is indisposed. Her next appearance in person is in Central Park tonight!" Slam went the phone.

The desk clerk winced as Seth emerged from the elevator and crossed the lobby to the street. The blowzy switchboard operator unplugged and turned to the desk clerk.

"That has-been's off her rocker. So help me Hannah she's off her rocker. Why doesn't somebody put her out of her misery?"

"Don't you give me that self-destructive applesauce, Barclay! This kid knows what she's doing! I got them all right here—right here in the palm of my lily-white hand!" She held the tiny talon up so that it reflected in the mirror. "I'm gonna bring them to their knees—begging, pleading, kissing the hem of my skirt. Then they'll do just like I tell them. They want me to lay off tonight? Fine! Then they do what I say. She's afraid to let me play her kid sister! That's why! She's afraid! She knows I'll walk off with the whole damn series, like that Ilya kid's snatching it right from under Mr. Solo's nose. Who the hell are *you* to warn *me?* Did *you* listen to *me?* Huh? *Huh?* You did *not!* And you got yourself killed for it like I said **you** would. Well, not this kid, big boy. This kid's gonna make headlines again if it's the last thing she ever does. The hell I'm frightened. The hell I am! You heard me telling that sap, didn't you? I got guts I ain't used yet. *"Tippy-tap-toe, Tippy-tap-toe, my favorite da-a-a-ance . . .'"*

"Flora."

"Yes, Fauna dear."

"You shouldn't have told Madeleine about Sweet Harriet's threat."

"We don't keep secrets from each other."

"I know, dear. But she doesn't seem to have the strength any more."

"I got all the strength we need, dear."

"She's worried about the boys. They're not in danger, are they, Flora?"

"I hope not," sighed Flora, "I hope not. I'm getting too old for this sort of thing."

"You're young in heart, dear, and that's what counts."

"You're right, sweetie. Now shut up and deal."

"Seth cat," sighed Pharoah into the phone, "I got a feeling you're in over your head."

"This kid, big boy," mimicked Seth as he winked at Ida, "can take care of himself."

Pharoah chuckled. Then: "Hear from the twin cats?"

"Had them up to our pad a couple of hours ago. It was love at second sight."

Pharoah twirled his key chain. "Mutual?"

"All the way, Pharoah cat. All the way. Seth baby really had it pegged right."

"Now, baby cat," cautioned Pharoah, "be careful. You're treading where angels fear."

"Ah, g'wan," jollied Seth, "you're just feeling left out."

"When I want to play this hand, snotty cat, I'll deal myself in."

"Anything on the Zelma Wave tracer?"

"Too early, cat. Three-hour time difference between

here and Frisco. And don't change the subject. You be careful."

"Promise and cross my heart. See you later." He hung up. "One very, very dry vodka martini on the rocks," he said to the bartender.

You're in over your head, Seth cat. Way over your head. There's more to this caper than you. There's me. Pharoah Love. Detective. The man who withheld evidence to save your neck. That gives them twin cats two aces for their hole. That hole could be big enough to hold two coffins. Seth cat, move over. Make room for Daddy Pharoah. He flipped the switch on his intercom.

"Send a teletype to L.A. Anything they've got on Peter and Robert Moulin. Capital M-o-u-l-i-n. Yeah, sweetheart, like in Moulin Rouge. Twins. Right. The kids that used to be in the movies. They're big boys now. Real big boys."

"The guttersnipe!" exploded Robert.

The blast did not succeed in shaking the desk clerk's foundation. "Sorry, gentlemen," smiling his desk clerk smile, "Miss Dimple is indisposed. Would you care to leave a message?"

"I'd love to," snapped Robert, "but I'm a gentleman. Come, Peter. Mr. Piro just might be waiting at Checkpoint Ida."

"Shit," growled Ida, "here comes Daphnis and Chloë."

Seth had seen Peter and Robert entering, through the mirror over the bar. He swiveled around on the stool and folded his arms over his chest. "You're early."

"The engagement," snapped Robert, "was canceled."

"Robert," said Peter softly, "I suggest we adjourn to a table."

"Of course. Does it matter where we sit, my good woman?"

Ida groaned inwardly. "There are thirty-three tables, my good man. Just choose whichever suits your fancy."

Robert selected a table in the rear of the room, and Ida brought them two daiquiris on the rocks without being asked. Peter's eyes lit up.

"You remarkable creature! You remembered what we drink!"

"I never forget a libation," Ida snapped, and returned to the bar.

"Spirited wench," commented Robert admiringly. "Now, then, are we correct in assuming you left Sweet Harriet in a bit of a state?"

"Lend an ear," said Seth, placing the miniature tape recorder on the table. "It's been rewound and waiting." He flicked the switch and the twins listened attentively to the conversation between Seth and Sweet Harriet.

"I'm gonna rock this town like it's never been rocked before. And you can tell that to Madeleine and Flora and Fauna and all the rest of your gang. Now *out!*"

"And with that," said Seth as the reel came to an end, "she shoved me out the door with a remarkable display of strength."

"The sort of strength it might have taken to cause Barclay Mill to plummet to his death?" Robert's question was mellifluously intoned.

Seth nodded. "And thirty-three years ago she was thirty-three years younger."

"Robert." Peter's temple was throbbing. "She knows who we are. Somehow, some way, I suspect she plans to use that information tonight."

"No, Peter." Robert was tapping an index finger against his cheek thoughtfully. "She's used Seth as a pawn. With her penchant for cheap melodramatics, she's assuming Seth will rush to the phone and alert Madeleine that the Indians are coming." Too late he wished he hadn't used the word "Indians," but if it bothered Seth his face didn't betray him. "Then she expects Madeleine will phone her, pleading with her to keep her silence, promising anything her childish, sad little heart desires. Who we are, Peter, is of no importance to that game little trouper. We're just supporting players in this little ghost story. Her threat is the exposure of Barclay Mill's murderer: An exposure that might very well destroy the tiny, untidy little group who've already suffered destruction in another era. How beautifully sinister this all is." He sighed. "It's Machiavelli and the Borgias all over again. Speaking of Borgias, another round of drinks?"

Ida caught their signal and nodded.

"Here's the way I see it." Seth sounded like a chairman at a board meeting. "We're dealing with six people conspiratorially involved in Barclay Mill's murder."

He began with his right-hand thumb. "Sweet Harriet."

Index finger. "Flora Fleur."

Middle finger. "Fauna Fleur."

Ring finger. "Sam Wyndham."

Pinky, and somehow most appropriate. "Sweet Harriet."

Left-hand thumb. "Zelma Wave. But my instincts tell me she's only on the periphery of all this."

"Clever murderers manage to remain peripheral." Robert wondered if Ida heard him as she arrived with the drinks. Her face was as bland and as innocent as a pickpocket.

"Something to nibble on?" she asked.

"We've sufficient food for thought," smiled Peter.

"Intellectuals," snorted Ida, waddling away. "What a load of shit."

Robert arched an eyebrow. "She doesn't pass judgment lightly, does she?"

"She's a doll," said Seth. Then he returned to the subject under discussion. "Stop me if I'm wrong, but I think it boils down to this: Every one of these six stands to suffer if Barclay Mill's murderer is exposed. Not one of them dares make a move. They live in fear of each other."

"Yes," said Robert, "I think you're quite right. They're a tightly woven tapestry. And somewhere there's a loose thread that can unravel it."

"Sweet Harriet." And Peter sipped his drink.

"Sweet Harriet," repeated Robert. "Seth, you haven't told Madeleine about Sweet Harriet's threat, have you?"

"Haven't spoken to her all day."

"Not a word, then. Let Sweet Harriet stew in her nimble juices. Let her sit alone, fretting, fuming, assuming her bluff has been called. Let her gorge rise until it erupts."

"And supposing," interjected Peter softly, "she comes to think better of it all before this evening's concert?"

"Well," exhaled Robert, "that's the gamble we're taking, isn't it? A toast," he said, lifting his drink. "Sweet Harriet."

The three glasses met and clinked in mid-air.

"Sweet Harriet," said Peter.

"The kid herself," contributed Seth.

"What's with them three?" the bartender asked Ida.

Ida shrugged. "Talking shop."

"Weally, Mummy? You weally mean it? You weally want to go tonight?"

"Yes, Frannie, yes yes yes." Zelma's eyes were feverishly bright, and Francis K. wiped the beads of perspiration from her forehead with his napkin.

"But, Mummy," Francis K. suddenly remembered, "it's damp at night in Centwal Pahk. Yaw athwitis might be excwooshiating."

"I want to be there. I want to be there with them. I want to be where there's a lot of people. Where there's a crowd. Where it's safe."

"Why ah you talking so stwange, Mummy?"

"I'm just excited, that's all. A tribute to your father's memory. We should be there."

Francis K. was finding her eagerness infectious. "A Cawey Cadillac, that's how we'll go, Mummy. In a Cawey Cadillac! We'll awwive in style, like the family of a celebwity should awwive! Let's spluhge this once, shall we, Mummy, shall we?"

"I'd like that, Frannie. I'd like that very much. I haven't been driven in a Cadillac in . . . Oh, God, what difference does it make?"

"Don't fwet, Mummy, please don't fwet. Theah's maw to life than fame and wiches. We have each othuh."

"That's right, darling," stroking his cheek as he lay his head in her lap, "we're better off than any of them. Much better off."

"That's wight, Mummy," purred Francis K. "It's just like deah sweet wonduhful Bette Davis said to Paul Henweid—'Why ask faw the moon? We have the stahs.'"

11

"The weather looks a bit threatening, Robert."

Robert joined Peter at the window and viewed the black cloud with a look of distaste he usually reserved for fifteen-cent hamburgers. "No fear, Peter. It's drifting northward. Target, we may safely assume, the Bronx." He returned to the wall mirror and continued adjusting his chartreuse Bronzini ascot.

Peter sank into an easy chair and lit a Tiparillo with a pencil-slim lighter. He watched the nimbus of smoke drift lazily toward the ceiling, then fell deep into thought, stroking his chin.

"Robert"—mouthing his brother's name in a tone that demanded attention—"it is later than we think."

Robert glanced at his wrist watch, then back to his brother's reflection in the mirror. "Nonsense, we've more than an hour."

"I'm not thinking about the concert. I'm thinking about us. We're in our thirties, and if we don't hasten our pace the parade will have passed us by." Robert finished admiring himself and crossed to the liquor cabinet, where soon the clink of ice against glass, the gurgle of Scotch inundating ice, and the hiss of a siphon alerted Peter.

"No daiquiris?"

"Alas, no. I forgot to replenish the rum." Robert crossed to Peter with the two Scotch-and-sodas and placed them on the coffee table. He sat on a hassock, lit a cigarette, and then looked into his brother's face.

"We agreed a long time ago marriage is out of the question until we know who we are. Neither one of us is a very good liar and wives are notoriously like beagle hounds when it comes to sniffing out untruths. Once we've located Mother, we'll sweat the truth out of her about Father, and then we can marry and become as commonplace as the majority of our contemporaries. Be nice if we could marry twins. Nonprofessionals, of course, though a musical aptitude and an appreciation of the arts are requisites. I couldn't tolerate a mate who didn't understand Antheil and Joan Miro."

"Where in God's name do we locate them?"

"I've given that a great deal of thought. We begin by placing an ad in the *Saturday Review* under 'Employment Opportunities.' Once we've made a satisfactory selection, we can arrange a double twin-ring ceremony and then possibly settle down in twin cottages in the Twin Lakes area, which I hear is quite beautiful. But first we have our mission to accomplish."

"You know," said Peter, "we should invite Seth to be our best man. Or will we each require one?"

"Why, Peter! That's never occurred to me!" Robert's look of astonishment gave way to one of amusement. "Our second best man could be Pharoah Love, couldn't it? That would certainly please James Farmer."

"Seriously. What about those two?"

"Love and Farmer?"

"Love and Seth. Does it strike you as a satisfactory relationship?"

"No," said Robert. "The hold they have on each other strikes me as more circumstantial than emotional. Look at how eagerly Seth accepted membership in our Cosa Nostra. I'm sure Mr. Love has been voicing his disapproval."

"A pox on Mr. Love," said Peter with an indifferent wave of his hand. "We're helping Seth become a useful member of the community. This morning I said his conscience is his cancer. I think we've helped stem the deterioration. Pharoah Love lacks the necessary sophistication to handle a man like Seth. He is, of course, his partner in crime. But that doesn't mean they have to expire of mutual suffocation."

"Poor Seth!" exclaimed Robert. "I *am* so *terribly* fond of him! Sad to realize it might be too late for him to realize his potential. He should have confessed his crime and hired Melvin Belli. However, that's neither here nor there." He glanced at his wrist watch. "Zero hour approaching. We can grab a sandwich at Chock Full o' Nuts."

"Oh, God," groaned Peter.

"Well, there's hardly time for anything Lucullan."

"That isn't what I meant. I was struck by a dreadful thought." The pained expression on Peter's face alarmed his twin.

"Peter? What's wrong?"

"The horror of it all! Supposing it turns out our dear Mama is the incredible Sweet Harriet!"

"Please, Peter. Not on an empty stomach."

"I didn't say I don't like them, cat, I don't trust them."

"You don't like them."

"I don't *trust* them."

"You hardly know them."

"I'll know them better in the morning." Pharoah admired the Windsor knot in his tie as Seth emerged from the bathroom.

"You've put a tail on them."

"No, cat." Pharoah grinned. "I know what they're up to here thanks to you."

"You're having L.A. check them out."

"Right on the button, baby cat."

"What the hell for?" Pharoah doubted Seth would hurl the military brush he was clenching in his right hand.

"For our protection, cat. I like to have a little reserve ammunition."

"Don't I know that!"

The grin was wiped from Pharoah's face. "Meaning?"

"You know damn well what I mean. I'm *suffocating*."

"You think you'd be breathing any easier in the pen?"

"That's the only frigging argument you've got!" shouted Seth. "Yes, I think I would breathe easier in a cell, come to think of it! I wouldn't have your fingers around my neck!"

"Horseshit! You come and go as you please."

"Not with you directing traffic! 'Where you been, baby cat?' 'Who you been with, baby cat?' 'Why so late, baby cat?' 'I don't trust *him*, baby cat,' 'I don't trust *her*, baby cat,' 'I don't trust *them*, baby cat.' Up *yours*, Pharoah cat!" He stormed into the bedroom and slammed the door shut.

The best laid plans of mice and men, said Pharoah to himself, often come awry. But I'm not a mouse and he's not a man and the fantasy of making a life with him that caused me to bind myself to his crime is now a nightmare. But he's all I've got. And I'm hanging on to what's rightfully mine, unless somebody jerks the rope and tightens that noose I'm positive is now around his neck.

Pharoah stared at the bedroom door. Not a sound from the other side.

"Cat? Hey, cat? Come on out. It's getting late. I'm sorry."

The silence depressed him, adding an unwanted weight to his heavy heart. He mustered up a grin and scratched at the door gently.

"Come out, come out, wherever you are. . . ."

Snap!
Crackle!
Pop!

The milk Fauna poured into the bowl was causing war among her Rice Krispies. Flora dropped something in the kitchen and Fauna suppressed a yelp. "What was that?"

"I dropped a stale bagel!" boomed Flora, entering with a plate of cold cuts. "Eat your cereal."

"I can't," said Fauna, pushing the bowl away, "I can't. Flora . . . let's not go to the concert."

"We have to, sweetheart." Flora bit into a slice of salami and studied the pale face at the opposite side of the table. "Eat the Krispies. It's been an exhausting afternoon and you'll need your strength."

"Oh, dear," sighed Fauna, "will our lives ever be uncomplicated? Will we ever realize the dream? You, me, Madeleine, together again? Is all this worth it? Really worth it?"

"It's worth it, all right." Flora smacked her lips as she rolled up a slice of ham. "You, me and Madeleine starring in one more picture together. We'll be high-kicking down them marble steps again, baby!"

"We won't be laughed at? We're not the kids we used to be."

"It's comeback time, baby. Everybody's making it. And you're still younger than most of them. We might even get Rick Drew back from that plantation of his in Hawaii. Look at how they eat us up on TV. They'll eat better with Cinemascope and stereophonic sound. Then I'll die happy."

"Things can still go wrong, Flora."

"Not now, baby. The marines have landed and have the situation well in hand."

"Supposing something goes wrong with Sweet Harriet."

"It won't. Try this ham. It'll melt in your mouth."

The green Chinese silk dress hugged Madeleine's body a bit too tightly, and momentarily she entertained the ugly thought of dieting. Come in, diet dear, trilled Madeleine. Come in and join Madeleine's tea party. Just take a seat among all those other ugly thoughts I've been entertaining. All my life, sighed Madeleine, all my life, ugly thoughts and ugly diets. Undernourished and oversexed. She stepped back from the floor-length mirror for a better perspective. It'll all work out. It always has. Why shouldn't it now? Why hasn't Sweet Harriet answered my message? Where the hell have Flora and Fauna been all afternoon? If that message Sam left me was all that urgent, why's *he* been out all day? Not a peep out of Seth or the twins. Well, I'll see them all tonight and God willing serenity will reign.

The phone rang and the silk rustled seductively as she crossed the room.

"Hello! Hello-o-o-o! *Hello-o-o-o-o!*"

"That's the way I like to hear my girl!" boomed Flora. "Full of spit and ginger and all cheery as hell!"

"Where've you both been all afternoon? I've been trying to get you."

"Oh, out and about. Hither and yon. A couple of department stores and a snack at Schrafft's. Good old Schrafft's. Can anything beat their sliced cucumbers and butter on dry gluten bread?"

"I thought you might like a lift to the concert."

"Naw, sweetie, we're gonna walk. Fauna wants a cocoanut-covered Good Humor and we can pick one up on our way into the park. What time are you getting there?"

"I'll be on time. Have you heard from Sweet Harriet?"

"Not since this morning."

"She's got me worried. I left her a message and she hasn't answered. That's not like her. I smell trouble."

"Stop sounding so worried. You got a big night ahead of you, baby. We cased the park on our way home and heard the orchestra rehearsing. Boy! What an arrangement of 'San Diego'! It ends with a twenty-four-gun salute. Somebody better warn them pigeons. Haw! Are you wearing the Chinese silk?"

"Yes. It's a little tight, but I can manage."

"Knock 'em dead tonight, baby, y'hear me? Knock 'em dead. For me and Fauna."

"For you and Fauna," echoed Madeleine. Everything for you and Fauna.

"See you then!" Flora boomed and hung up. "Come on, Fauna baby. A little more rouge on your cheeks."

"No," whispered Fauna, snapping the compact shut. "I'll look like a Kewpie doll."

"Then let's get moving," said Flora, grasping a large knitting bag. "Christ, how I hate concerts. Well," indicating the knitting bag, "this'll keep me busy when I get bored."

Fauna smoothed the front of her organdy dress with her black-gloved hands and then mustered a smile. "You know something, Flora?"

"What, baby?" asked Flora sweetly, holding open the door.

"It's almost like going to an opening at Grauman's Chinese."

"By Christ, baby, that's the spirit! Let's go. It's rendezvous time."

"I think she's gone out, Miss Cartier," said the blowzy blond switchboard operator into the mouthpiece.

"How long ago?" asked Madeleine. "Would you happen to know?"

"Hard to say, dear," the blowzy blonde said. "She's been in one of her peculiar moods today. I hope I'm not speaking out of turn, but I know you're such a good friend of hers."

What's wrong with me all of a sudden? Why am I trembling?

"Are you there, Miss Cartier?"

"Yes—yes, I'm listening." That dark cloud outside has disappeared. It's going to be a lovely clear night, out there under the stars. Or is there still a dark cloud hovering with an invisible cloak wrapped around it?

"Well, dear, twice the desk clerk had to go up and quiet her. You know. Yelling and shouting at somebody named Barclay."

Dear God!

"But the clerk said there was nobody in the room with her. Well, dear, then she got this phone call to that other friend of hers . . ."

Madeleine listened and what she heard made the blood curdle in her veins and her mouth go dry, and only later, in looking back on it in the stillness of her cell, did she understand the fearsome intuition that made her bolt from the room, fly down the hall, down three flights of steps, through the lobby and into the street, running toward Central Park as though the hounds of hell were baying and in terrifying pursuit.

"No answer," Seth said, and hung up. "That's very curious."

"Maybe we're stood up," said Pharoah, calmly buffing his nails.

"Come on," Seth snapped, crossing to the door, the earlier anger with Pharoah now being jostled by his irritation with Madeleine. "We'll go to the hotel directly. Well, come on, will you? It's late."

"Coming, O Great White Father. Pharoah's coming."

"Bastard," muttered Seth, and he crossed to the elevator, attacking the down button with his index finger as though he were gouging out an eye.

The meadow in Central Park where in another century sheep had grazed was now teeming with another form of animal life. A thousand people were seated in the rows facing the orchestra shell, and hundreds more were streaming down the aisles, cursing the earlier arrivals for having gobbled up the choicer locations.

Lad, A Dog sat on an aisle seat, patting the hand of the professorial-looking gentleman in the wheel chair. "Can you see all right, Mommy?"

"There's nothing to see yet," grumbled Lad, A Dog's uncle. "I want to go to a movie tomorrow. Take the afternoon off."

"Now, *don't* be unreasonable."

"I'm not! What's playing at the Bleecker Street Cinema?"

"*Citizen Kane.*" Lad, A Dog shrugged. "That's all they ever play."

A six-foot-tall cadaverous-looking female with a thick mane of black hair tied in a ponytail, wearing leopard-skin-tight leotards, and a black blouse shimmering with rhinestones, came past them with an entourage of five aesthetic-looking young men of various shapes, sizes and sexual preferences.

"Look," Lad, A Dog whispered excitedly, "Baby Lake Sturgeon!"

The musicians were beginning to file into the shell. Here a piccolo was tested, there an arpeggio on the harp. A clarinet squeaked and a trombone guffawed. The pianist hit a note and a dozen violins began tuning up. An army of crickets took advantage of the opportunity and began a tuning session of their own.

Countess Vronsky leaned forward and tapped Baby Lake Sturgeon's shoulder.

"Oh, hel-yo, Contessa," nasalized Baby Lake. She had a deviated septum, the least important of her many deviations. "Lee-ooks like a fee-un nay-ight, *n'est-ce pas?*"

"Why'd you stand up Sam Wyndham last night?" demanded the Countess.

"Had to go-ho to Ray-hay-mond's nee-yew under-huh-ground mee-ovie. *Cop-Pop-Op-Ulation.* Eigh-hate hours of two-hoo flea-hees bang-anging ea-heach other. A ma-hasterpiece."

The baldheaded Mr. Gordon of Sam Wyndham's Film Society sat with the wizened old Aileen Pringle enthusiast.

"I disagree with you completely, Edgar," huffed Mr. Gordon. "Bette and Joan were the *ne plus ultra* in *Baby Jane.*"

"That's a priori," retorted the wizened Edgar in his wizened-Edgar voice, "but it'd'a been a hell of a sight more interesting with Claire Dodd and Helen Vinson."

Uncle turned to Lad, A Dog and said testily, "Why'd you leave me home last night? I wanted to get a look at the Mill kid."

"You can get a look at him right now, Mommy," said Lad, A Dog, staring up the aisle. "Oh and goody goody! He's wheeling his mother—Mrs. Barclay Mill!"

Uncle-Mommy managed to turn around in his wheelchair. "The hell you say!" he muttered. "Don't you recognize her? That's Zelma Wave!"

"Where?" shrieked someone who had overheard.

"Who'd the old guy say she was?"

"Zelma Wave!"

"Zelma *Wave*? I thought she was dead."

Francis K. found a seat on the aisle and sat, arranging the blanket around Zelma's feet.

"All wight, Mummy?"

"I'm perfectly fine," said Zelma. "It's good to be out. Why's everybody staring at us?"

Francis K. looked around and recognized Lad, A Dog, Countess Vronsky, Mr. Gordon and several others. "They'uh looking at me, Mummy," said Francis K. shyly. "They wemembuh me fwom last night."

Lad, A Dog came hurtling up the aisle and knelt at Zelma's feet, clutching Uncle-Mommy's autograph book and a pen.

"Oh, please, Miss Wave. Please! Would you sign my mommy's autograph book? He just adores you."

Zelma was too startled to be confused by the double genders.

"Why, I . . ." she said, and then smiled. With difficulty she took the proffered pen in hand and carefully wrote her name in the album.

"You sneaky thing!" said Lad, A Dog coyly to Francis K. "Why didn't you tell us your mother was Zelma Wave?"

"Nobody asked," replied Francis K. ingenuously.

Mr. Gordon was craning his neck.

"Any sign of them?" cackled Edgar.

"Good heavens, no," said Mr. Gordon with a nervous twitch. "The reserved row is still empty. And there's not a sign of Sam Wyndham either."

Edgar sighed. "Them movie queens. They'd be late to their own funerals."

"Cliché, Edgar."

"Isn't everything nowadays?" rejoined the old man. "When's Sam scheduling that Gustav von Seyffertitz–Ferdinand Gottschalk double bill?"

"After the Jean Muir program. I hope he's got *Desirable* and *As the Earth Turns*. They're two of her best."

"Just got her autobiography from the lending library. Plan to dip into it when I crawl into bed tonight."

The conductor entered, and the audience applauded generously. He bowed, turned to the orchestra with his baton lifted, then, after a dramatic but not too effective pause, gave the downbeat.

A portion of the audience burst into applause as the familiar and slightly overarranged strains of "Tippy-Tap-Toe" assailed their ears.

"Do you see any of them, Robert?"

"No," whispered Peter. "But, of course, anyone could get lost in this throng."

"Lord in heaven above," sighed Robert, "did they *have* to open the program with *her* song?"

Flora and Fauna stood at the head of an aisle, holding each other's hand tightly.

"We'll walk to our seats when the number's over," whispered Flora, clutching the knitting bag.

"Flora," said Fauna weakly, "I feel faint."

"Buck up, baby. There's nothing to worry about."

Pharoah lit a cigarette while Seth paid the cab driver.

"Keep the change," said Seth as he straightened up and headed past the Good Humor man into the park. "That dizzy bitch Madeleine!"—pitching the words over his shoulder—"she's never pulled anything like this before."

Few people would have noticed the isolated little path that led off the main walk that connected with the sheep meadow. Certainly Madeleine, whose eye for small details was notoriously faulty, would ordinarily never have noticed it. But now her attention had been drawn to it. Now there was reason for her to follow the obscure little trail. It was dark and she was afraid of the dark sometimes, as she was afraid of snakes and rodents, but fear was furthermost from her mind now. No one saw her set foot on the little path. In the distance the concert was beginning, and that's where everyone was. If danger lurked behind the bushes that half obscured the little path, Madeleine gave no thought to it. A mental mugger was already attacking her heart, and it throbbed and pounded in agony.

And then she saw her.

Madeleine stood frozen, fists clenched and pressing her cheeks.

"Tippy-tap-toe, Tippy-tap-toe," drifted from the orchestra shell and dipped and curtsied and swirled about her.

There's nothing to be afraid of, Madeleine. There's nothing to be afraid of. You know her. You know her well. You know the white blouse and the accordion-pleated skirt. You recognize the initials over her left breast.

S.H.D. Sweet Harriet Dimple. The kid herself.

Say something, Madeleine. Say anything.

Sweet Harriet's iron-gray eyes were directed at the sky.

Her head was cocked to one side as though listening with pleasure to the not-too-far-away concert. Her mouth was open, perhaps in wonder, perhaps in surprise. And her tongue protruded, not in defiance, but because it had no choice.

There was a rope around Sweet Harriet's neck, and the rope was slung over the branch of a half-dead tree, and was tied to the trunk of an adjacent sapling.

The orchestra had reached the end of the first chorus of "Tippy-Tap-Toe," and a series of quiet but effective harp glissandos were suddenly and very amazingly drowned out by a series of not very quiet but tremendously effective shrieks.

Madeleine had found her voice at last, and piercing shriek after piercing shriek tore through the air, fell like blazing arrows and penetrated Seth and Pharoah and Flora and Fauna and Peter and Robert and Francis K. and Zelma and Countess Vronsky and Lad, A Dog and Uncle-Mommy and Baby Lake Sturgeon and three policemen and thousands of supporting players, and only Sweet Harriet Dimple paid it no heed, because she didn't have to.

She held center stage.

12

SETH AND PHAROAH were the first to reach Madeleine's side in the isolated little clearing where stood the strong little tree bearing its strange fruit. Madeleine was still frozen in position, fists tightly clenched and pressing against her cheeks, shriek after piercing shriek knifing the air mercilessly. Seth threw his arms about her, averting her head from the ugly sight, and the shrieks diminished into choking sobs. The police came up behind Pharoah, who promptly identified himself and the corpse. One officer rushed off to notify the precinct and the morgue. The other two officers were detailed to hold back the gathering crowd.

The policeman trying to restrain Peter and Robert from pushing past him heard Pharoah's authoritative "Let them through" and permitted the twins entrance to the inner if not too charmed circle.

Robert ran to Madeleine as Peter stood transfixed, staring at the swaying corpse, hand over his mouth to quell a rising nausea.

"Poor darling!" cried Robert. "Oh, my poor darling!"

Madeleine raised her head slightly, recognized Robert, and transferred away from Seth, arms around Robert's neck, face pressed against his chest, sobbing bitterly. Seth's attention was fixed on Pharoah and a policeman lowering Harriet's body. He didn't hear Peter come up behind him.

"Poor creature," Peter said, "she's tippy-tap-toed her last. Who found her?"

"Madeleine," said Seth quietly.

"Madeleine? What in heaven's name was she doing here?"

"When she's calmed down, they'll be asking her that."

As Sweet Harriet's body descended, Baby Lake Sturgeon, looking over the heads of the people in front of her, commented in an aside to her five escorts, "If An-handy War-haw-hol had seen tha-hat he'd have spi-hit with en-henvy!"

And in the sheep meadow the concert continued. Most of the audience had remained seated, either oblivious to or choosing to ignore the drama being played a few hundred yards to the west of them.

Lad, A Dog came tearing down the aisle and breathlessly panted the news to Uncle-Mommy. Uncle-Mommy clutched the crucifix that hung around his professorial neck and shook his head sadly.

"Martin," he said to Lad, A Dog, "let us pray."

Lad, A Dog knelt beside the wheel chair and lowered his head. Edgar, Mr. Gordon and Countess Vronsky clasped their hands and closed their eyes.

"Dear God up in heaven," spoke Uncle-Mommy, "take unto thee the soul of our dear departed artiste, Sweet Harriet Dimple. . . ."

The orchestra was rendering a spirited arrangement of "Keep Your Chin Up, America."

". . . Bless this lovely person who gave the world countless hours of happiness in a time of dire need. . . ."

"What's going on?" someone hissed in Countess Vronsky's ear.

She turned and fixed the infidel with a withering look. "We are praying for Sweet Harriet Dimple. She has gone to the big sound stage in the sky."

Zelma Wave neither heard the music nor felt her son's protective arm around her shoulder. Her eyes were glazed with a dull film of fear, and her arthritic hands lay limp in her lap.

"Mummy?" whimpered Francis K. "Shall we go home, Mummy?"

("I want to be there. I want to be there with them. I want to be where there's a lot of people. Where there's a crowd. Where it's safe.")

"Mummy! Mummy! Ah you all wight? What's wong,

Mummy? Mummy, speak to me! It's me! Fwancis K.!"

The news of Sweet Harriet's death spread through the crowd like a virus from row to row until it reached backstage and from there to the musicians, and came to rest with the conductor. He bowed his head, then tapped his baton briskly and addressed his ensemble.

"Let's do 'Tippy-Tap-Toe' again," he announced with a slight choke in his voice, "for Sweet Harriet."

He gave the downbeat, and "Tippy-Tap-Toe" achieved a new majesty.

"Dear God," groaned Seth, "must they play it again?"

"It's a tribute, cat," said Pharoah wryly, watching Peter applying the pencil-slim lighter to the cigarette Madeleine held in a trembling hand. Sirens announced the arrival of the police from Pharoah's precinct and the hearse from the morgue. Madeleine took a deep drag on the cigarette.

"There, Madeleine. That's better, isn't it?" Madeleine hugged Peter's concern to her bosom.

Her lips barely moved when she spoke. "Where's Sam?"

"I haven't seen him."

She took another drag on the cigarette. "Flora and Fauna?"

"I don't know, dear. Perhaps out there in the crowd. They may not know you're here."

Two morgue attendants passed them, carrying a stretcher, and Madeleine averted her eyes.

Pharoah was deep in conversation with two detectives from his precinct.

The medical examiner was kneeling beside the body and removing the rope from around Sweet Harriet's neck.

Robert stood alongside Seth. "I suppose suicide is a rather farfetched theory?" He wished he could reel the line back in and rephrase it. Madeleine had overheard and emitted a dry sob.

"It might have been, you know. It just might have been."

Pharoah and the detectives crossed to Madeleine. She faced them, folding her arms, making an effort to control her voice as she spoke.

"It was something the switchboard operator at her hotel told me earlier. It seems the desk clerk had to go up to S-S-Sweet Harriet's room on several occasions to quiet her this afternoon. She'd been screaming and carrying on, and . . . and holding . . . holding imaginary conversations with . . . with—" her eyes met Seth's— "Barclay Mill."

"Barclay Mill," Pharoah explained to the detectives, "is a Hollywood cat somebody murdered thirty-three years ago."

"Do we have to stay here?" cried Madeleine. "I'll be sick if I have to stay here another moment. Where's Sam, for God's sake? And the girls? I'm going to be hysterical again! I'm going to be hysterical again!"

She burst into tears and Peter put his arms around her.

"We'll need a statement from Miss Cartier," Pharoah said to Peter. "She found the body."

"Couldn't we go back to her hotel?"

Pharoah held a brief discussion with the detectives and then nodded to Peter. Seth and Robert caught Pharoah's signal and joined him.

"We're taking Madeleine cat to her digs. Join the party."

Reporters and photographers were swarming over the scene of the crime like ants at a picnic. Flashbulbs popped and hasty questions ricocheted around Madeleine's ears.

"Not now," Peter cried. "Not now! Miss Cartier is much too upset."

Flashbulbs continued to pop and Robert groaned to Seth, "They're getting her bad profile."

Several policemen forced an aisle through the curious crowd, and Madeleine was led out.

The morgue attendants lifted Sweet Harriet's body onto the stretcher. The iron-gray eyes remained fixed on the sky, unseeing, unappreciative, oblivious to the careful attention being paid, the attention so eagerly sought and never to be relished.

The orchestra played on.

Let's stick to-gether,
To-gether we don't fall a-part!

"Madeleine! Madeleine, baby! There she is, Fauna. Out of my way, flatfoot. The kid needs us."

"Flora! Don't leave me! Wait for me! I'm frightened!"

Flora grabbed Fauna's hand and pulled her past the policeman.

"Baby! What happened? What are you doing here?"

Madeleine stared into the anxious face. "Sweet Harriet is dead. Haven't you heard?"

"Yes," whimpered Fauna, "yes. And I saw it in her cards. I saw it in her cards!"

"Shut up, Fauna," Flora snapped. Hands on hips, she challenged the men surrounding Madeleine. "Where do you think you're taking her?"

"To my hotel," said Madeleine in a rasping voice. "They want a statement from me, *dear*—I found the body."

"What the hell were you— How awful for you, baby. Pull yourself together, Fauna. We're going to Madeleine's hotel."

"Go home," said Madeleine, eying the bag in Flora's hand, "and stick to your knitting."

"You need us!" boomed Flora.

"Go home and call Campbell's and arrange for Sweet Harriet's funeral."

"There's no rush," said a detective. "There'll have to be an autopsy first."

"Catch her! Catch her!" someone cried. "She's falling!"

Fauna slumped to the ground in a heap.

"Baby!" screamed Flora, kneeling and patting Fauna's wrist. "Baby! Somebody help my baby!"

"Oh, God!" cried Madeleine, clenched fists pounding her cheeks again. "I'm going mad!" Flashbulbs popped. "I'm going mad mad mad! Take me away from all this!

Peter! Robert! Seth! I'm going mad mad mad mad mad!"

"Isn't she marvelous!" said Mr. Gordon to Countess Vronsky. "When they created those girls they threw away the mold. They just don't make them like that any more."

A stranger blundering into Madeleine's suite would never have guessed a police investigation was under way. Madeleine sat in a Morris chair holding a glass of champagne, make-up refreshed and legs crossed seductively. Peter was pouring daiquiris onto rocks from a blender for Robert and himself. Seth sat in a window seat sipping a Scotch-and-soda. Flora held a snifter of brandy to Fauna's pale mouth, and Pharoah and the detectives were exchanging what appeared to be pleasantries. The newly arrived police stenographer marveled at the pleasant atmosphere as he waited to take Madeleine's statement.

Pharoah turned to Madeleine and silently admired her miraculous composure. "Shall we begin?" he asked pleasantly.

"We may as well," said Madeleine. "Shall I take it from the top?" For a moment her eyes met Flora's, then she sipped her champagne and spoke.

"I'd been worried about Sweet Harriet all day. I'd left a message for her at her hotel and she never replied to it, which was quite unlike her."

"When did you last see her alive?" asked the taller of the two detectives, Ed Mallory.

"Last night. At a Film Society showing of a film Sweet Harriet and I and they"—a listless wave in Flora and Fauna's direction—"appeared in. In our palmier days." Sam. Why wasn't Sam at the concert?

"Go on," prodded Mallory.

Madeleine rearranged herself and indicated that her glass needed refilling. Pharoah obliged, and Madeleine rewarded him with a faint smile.

"She seemed fine last night. In her glory, as a matter of fact. Surrounded by adoring fans and signing autographs. Detective Love and Mr. Piro can attest to that, can't you, boys? They had escorted me."

Mallory looked at Pharoah, who nodded.

"Then this afternoon I phoned her and left this message. Well, she never replied to it, and that was rather strange."

"Why?" asked Mallory.

"Sweet Harriet keeps in constant touch."

Fauna had found the strength to hold the brandy snifter cupped in both hands, and Flora was knitting at a scarf with a deftness that would have engendered envy in Madame Defarge.

"Now, then," said Madeleine, after a sip of champagne, "about an hour ago I finished dressing for the concert and was waiting for Mr. Piro and Detective Love, who were to escort me." Pharoah avoided Mallory's inquisitive glance. "I had some time to spare, so I decided to try Harriet again, thinking I might catch her before she left for the concert. That's when the switchboard operator told me about the trouble they'd been having with Harriet."

She repeated the details of Sweet Harriet's strange behavior.

"Well," continued Madeleine, "I just can't understand why, or how, or even what—call it woman's intuition—but when the operator told me she hadn't seen Harriet leave, I sensed something was wrong. You see, Harriet doesn't just enter or leave a place like ordinary people do. She . . . she . . . well, she's a bit of an exhibitionist. She . . . she tap-dances in public a great deal."

"She was off her rocker!" boomed Flora.

"Please!" Mallory snapped, and Flora dropped a stitch.

"Well, Flora happens to be right, Detective . . ."

"Mallory."

"Mallory. Really Mallory? Girls—remember Boots Mallory?"

"Would you please continue, Miss Cartier?"

Madeleine thought better of glaring at the tall detective, and went on with the narrative. "Well . . . I'd long suspected Sweet Harriet was off her—a bit unhinged, and I had this *terrible* premonition she might do something to herself." Her voice broke and she fumbled in her bosom and extracted a handkerchief and held it to her mouth briefly. She took another sip of champagne, and the police stenographer was madly in love with her.

"Where was I?" sighed Madeleine.

The stenographer reread her last sentence.

"Oh, yes. This sudden panic overtook me"—leaning forward in her chair ("We're dollying in for a close-up, Miss Cartier!")—"and, without even thinking of the boys coming to pick me up, I dashed out of the room. I didn't even wait for the elevator. I went careening down the stairs, through the lobby and into the street—everyone in the lobby must have thought I was *mad*. I don't know how I did it! I haven't run pell-mell in years. By the time I reached the park, the concert was under way. I was following the walk toward the music when . . . when . . ."

Click-click-click went Flora's needles, and Fauna peered into the snifter as though it were a crystal ball.

"Oh, dear *God!*" cried Madeleine. "Will you understand when I tell you? I had stopped to gain my bearings. I was alone. The walk was deserted and I suddenly felt afraid. And then . . . then I heard this sort of whimper, then a snap, like—oh, God, like a branch had been broken. And I turned, and I saw this little path half hidden by the bushes, and . . . and like some invisible magnet I was drawn to it. All I could hear was the sound of my own footsteps. Only the moonlight to light my way. And before I knew it, there she was . . . there she was, hanging there by the neck. And I started screaming. Oh, God, was I screaming!"

Pharoah stepped in. "That's when Seth and I heard her and found her."

"What an awful suicide!" sobbed Madeleine. "What a terrible way to kill herself!"

The sobs were interrupted by the ringing of the phone.

"Sam!" cried Madeleine. "It's got to be Sam."

Pharoah answered the phone.

"Pharoah Love here. Yeah, Barney. Let's have it."

Silence blanketed the room as Pharoah held the center of attention, listening carefully, occasionally nodding his head, twice grunting, "Uh huh," and finally saying, "Thanks, Barney," and hanging up.

"Well?" asked Mallory.

Pharoah stuck his thumbs in his vest and rocked slightly on his heels. "Coronor reports Sweet Harriet was already dead when she was strung up."

Seth heard a gasp and, without looking, assumed it was Madeleine.

"She was strangled to death. There were no injuries caused by the rope other than abrasions of the neck and chin."

Fauna's snifter crashed to the floor, and Flora caught her as she began to topple over.

"Fauna baby!" screamed Flora. "Fauna baby! Speak to me!"

Fauna baby lay stretched out on the couch with a cold towel on her forehead. Flora patted her wrists and Pharoah repeated an address into the phone. "Garden apartment. Sam Wyndham. W-y-n-d-h-a-m." He hung up and turned to Madeleine as she entered from the bathroom with a fresh wet towel in her hands.

"Madeleine cat, we're going to have to stick around here until we locate the Wyndham cat."

"I'd like to ask him a few questions myself," boomed Flora. "He and Sweet Harriet had a knock-down drag-out at his place today."

"How'd you know that?" asked Loeb, the smaller of the two detectives.

"Straight from the horse's mouth. Sweet Harriet told me herself."

"When was this?" asked Loeb, brows furrowed.

"She phoned me just after lunch today in a shit snit."

"Why didn't you tell us she had contacted you?" asked Mallory.

"Because nobody asked me, flatfoot."

Fauna moaned. Madeleine switched towels but was unsuccessful in her attempt to catch Flora's eye. Seth, holding the knitting bag in his lap, sat on the windowseat alongside Robert. Peter stood leaning against the wall next to Robert.

"What exactly did Sweet Harriet say to you?" they heard Mallory ask.

"I can't remember her exact words," Flora said, "but all she kept saying was things like 'If he thinks I'm afraid of him, he's got another guess coming, kiddo' and things like that. Then she said a lot of terrible things about everybody."

"Like who?" asked Pharoah.

"Like Madeleine and me and poor Fauna here."

Fauna's eyes were opened.

"You feeling better, baby?"

"Yes, Flora." Fauna's voice was strange, different, almost disembodied.

"You four girls get along O.K.?" asked Mallory.

"Why, Sweet Harriet and us have been buddies for years!" Flora roared, and Mallory's ears quivered. "And let me tell you, Buster, she ain't been all that easy to get along with."

"Why was that?" asked Loeb quietly.

"Because she was a big pain in the ass." Flora segued into a capsule biography of Sweet Harriet's burning desire for a return to the limelight, capped by the events that led to Sweet Harriet's arrival in New York and her Wednesday exhibitions on Broadway between West Seventy-second and West Seventy-third.

Madeleine was back in her chair sipping champagne, and Robert's attention had been directed by Seth to the interior of the knitting bag.

"How'd she support herself?" asked Mallory.

"I supported her."

All eyes were on Madeleine.

"I couldn't let her starve to death." "Death" hung in mid-air for a few seconds before expiring. "I'm a rich woman and she was a good friend. I gave her a weekly allowance. One hundred dollars."

Somebody whistled. Pharoah shot a look at the stenographer, who hung his head, abashed.

Madeleine shrugged. "Well why not? In this day and age it's a mere pittance. I've often contributed sums to the girls here, haven't I, girls?"

"She's got a heart as big as a producer's ego," offered

Flora. "Madeleine's the best. Let me tell you that. The best."

"The best," echoed Fauna faintly, and Flora winked at her and pinched her cheek.

"I want to sit up," said Fauna, and Flora moved to one side.

Once Fauna was in a sitting position: "I'd like some more brandy, please." Peter crossed to the sideboard and poured a snifter of brandy.

"I'm a very wealthy woman," Madeleine said, drawing all the attention to where she wanted it. "I even help Sam Wyndham out when he needs it. He's my ex-husband," addressing the detectives, "in case you haven't already known the fact. I don't mind," she added with a rueful shake of the head. "These people worked to get me to the top of the heap and keep me there. I couldn't refuse them a thing, could I?"

Fauna accepted the snifter from Peter with a faint "Thank you," then startled him by downing the contents in four gulps.

"Easy, baby, easy," cautioned Flora.

Out of the corner of his eye Pharoah studied Seth and Robert, who had their heads together. He wished it were tomorrow, when the report on the twins from L.A. might be on his desk.

"Is anybody hungry?" trilled Madeleine. "I haven't had a thing to eat and I'm famished. Seth, be a darling and get room service to send up a tray of sandwiches and coffee. Well, will you look at those two! So fascinated by Flora's knitting bag!"

Flora crossed the room in five thudding strides and snatched the bag from Seth's hands. "Why didn't you tell me it was in your way?" In five thudding strides she was back seated alongside Fauna.

"I'd like more brandy, please," requested Fauna. Flora shot her a startled look as Peter crossed to her with the bottle and poured.

"Take it easy, baby," cautioned Flora.

"Oh, I'm fine now," whispered Fauna, "absolutely fine! I've had a vision, you know, and everything's going to be just fine."

Pharoah hovered over Seth and Robert.

"What's with the knitting bag, cats?" he sotto-voced.

"Patience, cat." Seth smiled, rising and heading for the phone. "We were just admiring a cross stitch."

Robert chuckled, rising and crossing to the sideboard.

Temper, Pharoah cautioned himself, temper, cat. All things come to him who waits.

"Murder!" Was that Lady Macbeth or was that Madeleine, Robert wondered as he turned.

"Good God," cried Madeleine, "it's just striking home! Sweet Harriet was *murdered*. We're *suspects!* This is an *investigation*. There'll be reporters and headlines and *scandal!* Ha ha ha ha ha ha ha ha!"—head flung back and laughing uproariously. "Madeleine Cartier rides again. You know what that means, girls?"

Fauna paled and Flora's face was a sodden mask.

"It's the kiss-off, sweethearts! Goodbye, TV series! There it goes—" her right hand made lazy circles—"right up the flue. I'm free, by Christ, I'm free!"

13

THE BRAVE LITTLE WOMAN barring the two policemen's way was probably in her early sixties, but the determined, defiant face belied the frailty of her years. The bulldog cast to Mrs. Crosman's face had developed over her thirty years as a landlady, thirty years of coping with hundreds of individual adversaries, her lessees. She had been challenged by the police before, and though she knew that soon she would relent and admit them to Sam Wyndham's apartment, she would continue to relish the role of embattled warrior and play her brave defiance to the hilt.

"Listen, lady," reasoned Lindsay, the younger of the two policemen, "we been ringing that doorbell and banging on the window for over ten minutes. Now, there's a light on in there and I hear a radio playing. That means somebody's in there. Anybody live here besides Sam Wyndham?"

"No!" she yapped.

"Is there a back way out?"

"No!" Yap.

"He may be sick. He may be hurt. He may be dying. We been sent here to get him."

"He's probably drunk." Yap yap yap.

The older policeman, Wagner, stepped between them.

"Listen, missus, you gonna open that door or ain'tcha? Because if you ain't, we'll force entry—"

"Against the law!" Yap yap yap. "I know my rights."

"We got orders to bring this guy in," said Lindsay with admirable patience. "Don't you know it's fashionable to cooperate with the Police Department these days? Come on, now. Open it up for us. You'll come in with us, see.

And if he ain't to home, you'll see that nothing's disturbed. Then we can report back and say he's not here. Then we've done what we've been told to do. Don't that make sense?"

"What's he done?" she asked, eyes narrowed.

"We don't know, lady," said Wagner. "We just been told to pick him up and deliver him to a certain hotel over on the West Side. Now, come on, willya? You don't want us to get our behinds chewed off, do you?"

"You belong in the subways," she yapped. "That's where you're needed, in the subways."

With relief, Lindsay and Wagner watched her insert the passkey into the lock and open the door. They followed her in.

"Keeps a neat and tidy place, for a lush, don't he?" said Mrs. Crosman with a display of pride. "Not a bad tenant, really. Except when he runs old movies late at night and I have to phone down to tell him to lower the volume. Asks me in sometimes to look at them with him. He's got the big bedroom down the hall fixed up with a movie camera and shelves of old films reaching to the ceiling."

Lindsay and Wagner headed down the hall, Mrs. Crosman trotting at their heels.

"This it?" asked Lindsay, indicating a door.

"Now, just wait a minute. Maybe that's why he didn't hear us. Stand aside."

She rapped at the door.

"Mr. Wyndham? You in there?"

The pressure of her knock caused the unlatched door to swing slowly ajar. Mrs. Crosman poked her head in the room.

"Mr.—"

She yelped and backed out with hands over her eyes. The policemen rushed in.

The room was exactly as Mrs. Crosman had described it. A sixteen-millimeter projector stood against a wall. On the opposite wall hung a small white screen. There were shelves that reached the ceiling, and against one set of shelves stood a ladder. At the foot of the ladder lay what seemed to be at first a crumpled heap of clothing.

Lindsay and Wagner knelt at Sam Wyndham's side.

One leg was folded under the other. His right hand clutched a rung of the ladder. His left was slightly frozen in air, fingers clenched and stiffened with rigor mortis. The color of his face was an ugly blackish purple. His eyes were open and his tongue protruded from his mouth. The head lay cheek against the floor, and even Lindsay could guess the neck had been broken.

Wagner exhaled. "Must have taken quite a tumble. I'll call the precinct on the radio." He got to his feet, passed the weeping landlady in the hallway, made his way to the street and the police car outside, and relayed the information that Sam Wyndham was dead.

"Shall I bwew us some tea, Mummy? Shall I?" The little-boy voice pleaded for attention. "Shall I, Mummy? Shall I bwew the tea?"

Zelma sat in the wheel chair, eyes fixed on the television set, waiting for the late night news.

"I'll bwew the tea, Mummy. You'll feel wefweshed aftuh you've had some tea."

Zelma should have been startled and pleased that her son had finally made a decision of his own, but she was too paralyzed with fear to notice.

"Mummy—*please!*"

"What *is* it, Franny?"

"Shall I bwew some *tea?*"

"God, no. Get me a drink."

"But the doctuh said you shouldn't. It's bad for yaw ahthwitis."

"I want a *drink*. And check the door again. Make sure it's locked tight."

"I've checked it thwee times aweady."

"Check it again. Check it again, Franny. I'm afraid, baby. I'm afraid."

"But *why?*"

"Somebody thinks I know something. And I don't, I don't," she sobbed. "But how do you convince a maniac? Poor Harriet. Poor Sweet Harriet."

"Dweadful. Such a howendous way to commit suicide."

"She was murdered, Franny. She was murdered. You wait and see. It'll be on the evening news. I know it will. Oh, God, I can't stand that soap opera. Turn down the sound. Abortions! Rape! Incest! They call that life? Life!" The laugh that followed was dry and worn, and it made Francis K. wring his hands.

"Suicide. It's Barclay's murder all over again. Trying to call it a suicide. Well, they won't quash it this time. There are no powerful studios to quash it for them now. Will you for Christ's sake get me that drink? And stop wringing your hands! You look like Lillian Gish."

I've been to many a wake in my lifetime, thought the police stenographer as he attacked his second turkey sandwich, but none as delightful as this. He stirred his coffee and contemplated the others contentedly.

Madeleine had changed to a hostess gown and was hovering over Flora and Fauna as she nibbled a gherkin. Mallory and Loeb ate sandwiches and sipped coffee and conversed quietly. Pharoah sat on the window seat with Seth and Peter, and Robert sat cross-legged on the floor. Pharoah was wondering how to wrest the knitting bag from Flora's beefy hands without causing a volcanic eruption.

"No use rushing it," said Pharoah. "We'll wait till the boys bring Wyndham here." He glanced at his wrist watch, and Seth recognized the impatience in his face.

"Fauna baby," said Flora with motherly concern, "that's your seventh brandy."

"I can count, Flora," replied Fauna in a voice more appropriate to a ventriloquist's dummy.

"Stop avoiding my question, Flora." Madeleine spoke under her breath. Her words were for Flora alone, and the two detectives were within earshot.

"Cut it," snapped Flora. "This is not the time for it."

"I want to know before Sam gets here."

Flora laid the knitting bag aside, and at the other side of the room Pharoah looked up alertly.

"Fauna and me are clean," whispered Flora with admirable effort. Whispering did not come easily to her.

The last time she had whispered in a movie theater, a man twelve rows behind had asked her to shut up.

"Stop talking in circles."

The phone was nearest Mallory, who picked it up when it rang. "Mallory."

Madeleine moved away from the sisters, and the peculiar look on Mallory's face gave her a sinking feeling. Pharoah had moved to Loeb's side, and the twins had risen from the floor. Seth stared at Madeleine and heard the muted echoes of "I'm free, by Christ, I'm free!"

"O.K.," said Mallory heavily, "get the coroner's report" —Madeleine gasped—"to me as soon as you can. Yeah. I'll wait here. May as well." He hung up.

"What's up?" asked Pharoah.

Mallory scratched his head and entertained an irresistible urge to chuckle.

"Was that about Wyndham?" persisted Pharoah.

"Yeah. . . . Yeah, Pharoah," giving in to the urge and chuckling like the putt-putt-putt of a motorboat, "that was about Wyndham. Seems the son of a bitch fell off a ladder and broke his neck."

Slowly Madeleine sank into the Morris chair, the champagne spilling over and staining the sleeve of her gown.

Seth heard someone whimpering and stared at Fauna.

She wasn't whimpering at all. She was giggling. "I saw a skull in my teacup today," she tittered. "I use Tetley's tea, because their leaves have individual personalities. You didn't know that tea leaves are highly individualistic, did you?" She was speaking to no one in particular. She spoke in short, mechanical jerks, like a talking doll operated with a hand crank. "There are no two leaves alike. They are as individual as the letters in an alphabet. That's why they can be read. Their code is a simple one to decipher," she continued, like a eugenics professor delivering a lecture. "I saw a skull in my teacup today." She settled back against a pillow with a smug expression on her face, not realizing Flora had removed the snifter from her hand and was draining it.

Loeb broke the silence. "Do they want us there?"

"Not necessary," said Mallory. "The Chief sent Sanders."

Why do my cheeks feel so damp? thought Madeleine. Are those tears trickling out of my eyes? If they are, why aren't I sobbing? Why are the twins staring at Flora and Fauna that way? Why is Seth sitting with his hands clasped so tightly together?

"Sam must have been drunk!" she blurted, sounding like an opera star trying to lend conviction to a line of dialogue. "He must have been drunk and lost his balance and toppled over and . . ." Her voice broke. Was that me speaking? No it couldn't have been. It was somebody else who said those words. When was it? Yes! Thirty-three years ago! Whose arm is that around my shoulder? Flora? Yes. That's right. That's how we played the scene then. Flora had her arm around my shoulder and she said he must have been drunk and lost his balance and toppled over.

"Isn't that so, Flora?" she implored with the innocent eyes of a fourteen-year-old. "Isn't that what you told me the next morning?"

"Baby, baby, baby," said Flora over and over again. "My poor baby."

Madeleine slapped her arm away and jumped to her feet, staring down at Flora, fists clenched, face purple with rage.

"But I saw it, dammit! I saw it myself! That wasn't the way it happened at all! He didn't lose his balance!"

"Dear God!" gasped Peter. "She's in shock!"

"She talking about Wyndham?" Mallory asked Pharoah.

"No." It was Seth speaking. "She's talking about Barclay Mill."

"The cat I was telling you about," said Pharoah to Mallory and Loeb. "Barclay Mill. Found dead in his Hollywood mansion thirty-odd years ago, lying at the head of a stone staircase leading to his swimming pool. Neck broken. Presumably fell from a terrace. These ladies were mixed up in it."

Flora stared at Pharoah and wondered when he had

found the opportunity to appropriate her knitting bag. "Give that to me!" she ordered sternly, rising to her feet. "Give me that knitting bag."

"Sorry, Flora cat," handing it to Mallory, "it's heading for the Police lab."

> "Tippy-tap-toe,
> Tippy-tap-toe,
> My favorite da-a-a-ance!"

sang Fauna in a frail wisp of a voice.

> "Tippy-tap-toe,
> Tippy-tap-toe,
> Come on! Take a cha-a-ance!"

"Give me that knitting bag."

"It should have been my song," Fauna said, sitting up abruptly, "but she made Barclay take it away from me and give it to her. I could have killed her! I could have killed her!"

"You listen to me, flatfoot!" shouted Flora. "You know what happened. It's easy as pie. Sweet Harriet and Sam had a fight. He followed her to the park, killed her and strung her up to make it look like suicide. Then he went home and got pissy-eyed drunk and fell off that ladder."

"No, Flora, no," said Seth, "that's not the way at all."

"Give me that knitting bag!" she shrieked, hurling herself at Pharoah with projectile force. "You ain't pinning this on me."

Pharoah lay on the floor, and Flora straddled him in one swift movement, powerful, beefy hands squeezed tight around his neck. Mallory and Loeb rushed at her, Mallory twisting his arm around Flora's neck in a powerful grip, Loeb struggling to free her fingers from Pharoah's windpipe.

"You're hurting her!" Madeleine screamed. "Boys! Don't let them do that to her!"

Fauna hummed to herself and danced around the room, her hands lithely extended, oblivious to the drama in the center of the room co-starring Flora and Pharoah.

Madeleine rushed at Mallory and Loeb, hands clawing the air, intercepted by Peter and Robert. The police stenographer sat transfixed, mouth agape, breathing in short asthmatic wheezes. He planned to dine off this evening for months to come. Peter and Robert forced Madeleine back into the Morris chair, where she continued to struggle.

Seth never moved. The sight of Pharoah's bulging eyes and the sound of his painful gasps as he gulped for air held him hypnotized. He felt giddy and lightheaded and was momentarily filled with an elation he hadn't known in months. She almost had him. *Another second and I might have been staring at a dead cat. I'd have been free, by Christ, I'd have been free!*

"Goddam mother-grabbing flatfoot bastards!" screamed Flora.

Mallory held her hands pinned behind her in a steel-like grip as Loeb helped Pharoah to his feet. Fauna pirouetted past them and lit at Seth's feet. She took hold of his hands and kissed both palms. Then she released his left hand and stroked his right palm.

"I saw death here, that's what I saw," she whispered. "That's what I couldn't tell you yesterday. Just like that gypsy did with Noël Coward in *The Scoundrel*. I saw death and didn't want to tell you. And it's still there. It's still there." With the grace of a nymph playing tag with Pan, she moved away from him and flew to Madeleine's side, studying the weeping woman with a look of beatific sympathy.

"Dry your eyes, Madeleine darling," she whispered drunkenly, "dry your eyes. We have wept too much, we three. I for one," she said gaily, "shall enter a plea of insanity."

There wasn't a soul in the room who hadn't heard her.

Madeleine looked up abruptly. Peter dropped Madeleine's left hand and Robert released the other and Flora stopped struggling. The police stenographer wished his heart wouldn't thump so loudly, while the others watched with horror and fascination as Fauna did Sweet Harriet's familiar thirty-second-time step, ending on her knees at Flora's side.

"We leaped before we looked, didn't we, darling? The way we always did. There'll be no TV series now. There'll only be another scandal and they'll be talking about Barclay again and Madeleine's career is finished forever and the three of us shall never appear in another movie together—and I knew it all the time. I saw it in the cards and I never told you. I should have told you, Flora, shouldn't I have told you?"

Her knees gave way and she sank to the floor, her cheek nestling Flora's like a tiny puppy's, humming "Keep Your Chin Up, America."

"Let go of me, flatfoot," Flora said to Mallory, "and I'll wrap it up for you."

"Let her up," said Pharoah.

Mallory relaxed his grip, moved to one side, and Flora sat up. Fauna moved her head to Flora's lap, and one beefy hand stroked her hair affectionately.

"Well? Aren't there any gentlemen present? Give me a cigarette, somebody."

Robert crossed to Flora, cigarette case extended and open, and she selected one. Peter sat next to Flora, holding the pencil-thin cigarette lighter, and she took a deep drag, exhaled, and smiled at Madeleine.

"Everything, baby?"

"Everything, Mother."

Peter dropped the cigarette lighter.

14

"MOTHER!" exclaimed Robert.

"You can say *that* again!" boomed Flora.

"Yes, Mother!" A defiant pride was in Madeleine's voice as she crossed to the couch, wedging herself in between Peter and Flora, an arm around Flora's shoulder and kissing her cheek.

Fauna sat up and smiled across the room at Seth. "Didn't you ever suspect, Mr. Piro? I was positive you did."

Seth shook his head dumbly. "I told Flora I thought you might have guessed. Madeleine's my baby sister. She's four years younger than I am. She was at school back East when Barclay signed Mother and me for pictures. Mother was married when she was fifteen, and I was born two weeks later, wasn't I, Mother? In Chillicothe."

"That's right, dear," said Flora, patting Fauna's head. "Now let Mother do the talking." She addressed the room. "Her father was a quick-change artist in vaudeville and I was an acrobatic dancer. We were part of a unit traveling the Gus Sun time. A few months after Fauna was born her father disappeared, and later I learned he was shot and killed during a crap game in New Orleans. They caught him switching the dice. Poor Izzy. That was his last quick change. Then I joined a Fanchon and Marco unit and met Madeleine's father. He was a tenor. Bob Peters. I can still hear him singing 'Roses Of Picardy.' You could almost smell them roses, the way he sang it. Anyway, Madeleine was around ten years old when Bob had a heart attack onstage at the Majestic Theatre in Brooklyn. Somebody in the balcony yelled

'Encore!' and it was too much for him. He just keeled over. I put Madeleine in school, and Fauna and me became the Fleur Sisters. I was almost thirty then, but I looked sixteen. I'm in my late sixties now." She winked at Seth. "Would you ever guess it?"

"Never, Mother, never," Madeleine said, patting her hand.

Flora smiled. "That's my baby. Then along came Barclay, scouting acts, and Fauna and me were in a prologue at Grauman's Chinese. We were Arabian houris—them's dancers, boys—because the picture was about an Arabian prince."

"*Fazil*," said Fauna.

"Yeah, baby. *Fazil*. Charlie Farrell and Greta Nissen. Poor Greta. That Swedish accent killed her in squawkies. Well, anyway, I was a pretty *zoftig* kid then and Barclay was eating me up with his eyes all the way up there in the loge. One thing leads to another, and him and me become lovers. The next thing you know, we're in the *Follies of '29*. I won't bore you with the more gruesome details. There's also Sweet Harriet, and I get the kiss-off, but I don't give a damn. We got a five-year contract, and the Smollett Brothers got their eye on Fauna for star material. That's when I get it in the back of my mind to bring Madeleine out to the Coast in a couple of years and get her going in pictures too. Sweet Harriet and Barclay go at it hot and heavy for a while and it's sort of an on-and-off affair for a couple of years, by which time Fauna and me gets kind of friendly with Harriet. She's only a kid then, you got to remember, and not the mean and vicious bitch she was up until a couple of hours ago. And all the time there's Sam Wyndham, Barclay's chief cameraman, and Sam's beginning to say to me, 'Hey, kiddo, better get some sleep—lot of telltale lines showing around your eyes,' and it kind of gets me worried, like maybe my days in pictures are getting numbered, because you can't lie to the goddam camera. So I make up my mind to get my kids on top, and then I'll fade into the background. So I send for Madeleine, and Christ, was she a beauty!"

"What about Zelma Wave?" asked Seth.

"What about her?"

"Didn't any of you know then she was married to Barclay?"

"Never even guessed it. Didn't know till she started shaking Madeleine's tree back in 'thirty-five."

"Zelma's been very frightened," said Madeleine.

"Ah, that water buffalo was always frightened. Listen, who's telling this story?"

Madeleine sighed. "You are, dear."

"You bet your ass. Say! Great title for a quiz show. Anyway, behind my back Fauna and Barclay are having a go at it. Sweet Harriet finds out and spills the beans to me and I blow my top and go to Barclay and threaten to blow his. So he tells me to lay off or Fauna's finished in pictures. Well, have you guys ever heard of Mother Love? That's what I'm consumed with. Mother Love. I want my babies to make it to the top, 'cause all we got is each other. And now I got Madeleine with me, too, and I fix it so Barclay manages to 'discover' her too."

Madeleine was at the champagne cooler, filling her glass.

The public stenographer's fingers were racing to keep up with Flora's machine-gun narrative. Pharoah leaned against the wall near the couch, arms folded, listening to Flora and eying Seth. What's that peculiar look on baby cat's face, he wondered. Why does he keep avoiding my eyes?

"Then something happens I didn't figure on," he heard Flora say. "Fauna tells me Barclay's promised to marry her, and Sweet Harriet tells us she's heard he's got a new kitten curling up in his bed."

"Me." Madeleine raised her glass in a silent toast and drank.

"Yeah," said Flora sadly, "Madeleine. Sweet Harriet knew it was Madeleine, but didn't tell us at the time. You see, when Madeleine first hit Hollywood we made it look like we didn't know each other. Then, gradual like, we went through the routine of becoming friendly on the set and then taking her under my wing because she was just a kid who needed friends and protection. But Fauna had made a mistake. She got drunk at Barclay's one night and told him Madeleine was her sister and they were both my kids, and that was all Barclay needed. He'd been making passes at Madeleine and getting noplace. When he threatened Madeleine he'd expose us all, he got where he wanted. Madeleine gave in."

"That experience," announced Madeleine grandly, "was responsible for my subsequent traumas. Men, scandal, men, scandal, men, scandal. An erotic Catherine wheel."

"Now," said Flora darkly, "we come to the night Barclay got his." She spit Barclay's name like the residue of a plug of chewing tobacco. "Here's what really happened that night." She looked at Seth, then at Pharoah. "Madeleine told Fauna and me you guys got your hands on the L.A. file about Barclay's murder. Well, them statements we gave were a lot of horse manure. *I*"—booming with pride as she pounded her chest—"made up that whole story we gave the cops. What really happened was this. . . ."

Peter and Robert were staring at Madeleine. She sat at the edge of the Morris chair, eyes fixed on the carpet.

"Barclay asked Fauna to come for dinner all right, but what she didn't know was that Madeleine was already there."

"What's all this got to do with the murder of Sweet Harriet and Sam Wyndham?" asked Mallory impatiently.

"I'm getting there!" snapped Flora.

"Leave strangler cat be," said Pharoah. "She's bringing us to the end of the rainbow."

"Yeah," sighed Flora, "the end of the rainbow. Well, like Sweet Harriet said, she was supposed to be there to borrow these here French grammars 'cause she's got this offer to go to France and do a movie with some frog tenor—"

"Henri Garat," interjected Fauna. "Fox brought him to America for a movie with Janet Gaynor. *Adorable.*"

"Yeah, he was cute."

"No, Flora. That's the name of the movie."

"Sure, baby. Anyway, Sweet Harriet gets there earlier than she's expected. They don't hear her coming in. And she overhears this scene between the three of them. Madeleine's sitting on the terrace swing—"

"Crying my eyes out," said Madeleine.

"Yeah. And Fauna and Barclay are having a knock-down drag-out."

"He was very drunk," whispered Fauna.

"Yeah. And Barclay hits Fauna."

"That made me very mad," whispered Fauna, "and I *screamed* at him. Madeleine jumped out of the swing and came running to me, but she was too late. Oh, she was much too late. Barclay came at me again, but I charged at him like a young bull, and wheeeeeeeeee! Over he went! And we heard the thud, and neither one of us dared look. And that's when Sweet Harriet walked in and said, 'Well, kiddo, it's curtains for you.' She had seen me kill Barclay."

"You didn't kill him." Flora dropped her cigarette on the floor and crushed it with the heel of her shoe. "Tell them, Madeleine."

Madeleine handed her empty glass to Peter and got to her feet and began pacing the room. "Harriet said she wouldn't tell anyone if Fauna would turn down the big movie she was supposed to star in on her own. Sweet Harriet wanted it that badly. I happened to be looking down at Barclay and—and I saw him move. He wasn't dead at all. He was injured, but he wasn't dead. I told Sweet Harriet that Fauna couldn't make a decision without Flora."

"Okay, kiddo," said Sweet Harriet, hands on hips and tapping one foot impatiently, "get Big Sister over here and on the double! I can handle the three of you." With the thirty-second-time step for emphasis.

Flora took over again.

"Madeleine phoned me, and I was there in ten minutes. She'd told me about Barclay and I came in around the back. They were up on the terrace and didn't see me.

I went straight to Barclay and he was coming to." She clenched and unclenched her beefy fingers as her eyes locked with Fauna's. "I'd had plenty of time to think, driving to Barclay's, and I made my decision when I pulled into the driveway. I was going to fade out of pictures and leave the field clear to my babies. But first Barclay had to go, before he loused them up. I broke his neck." She snapped her fingers. "It was easy. It was a skinny little neck. Then I headed up the stairs to the terrace. Sweet Harriet had been standing at the head of the stairs watching me. You have to hand it to the little bitch. She wasn't afraid. She didn't flinch. She just stood there smiling. . . ."

"Thanks, kiddo. Now I don't have to go do no movie in Paris. That was Barclay's way of trying to put the squeeze on this kid. He was trying to finish me. Thanks, kiddo. Thanks a big bunch o' bananas!"

"That's when we made the deal with each other. We'd quit Hollywood and then she'd get the lead in every musical the studio had lined up. There was money involved, too. She was up to her ears in hock and knew I'd been stashing away half our earnings every week. Right then and there in Barclay's bedroom, I put it all in writing and made Sweet Harriet sign it, so if she ever opened her mouth she'd be up to her neck in it as an accessory. She signed all right. Then we figured out what we'd tell the cops, and I took Fauna and Madeleine home to our place—Madeleine had been living in a small place of her own. Sweet Harriet waited half an hour before calling the cops. That's all the time she needed to find the letters Fauna and me and her and a couple of others had written Barclay. Well, you know what happened. All of us, except Madeleine, was smeared over the front pages of every newspaper across the world. The studio suspended us, including Harriet, and she didn't count on that happening. That's when she decided to sell the letters, thinking they'd make her name box office again. The dumb bitch. The studio spends a fortune quashing the whole story so there'd be no murder investigation, and she goes and sells the damn letters. That killed us forever. Fauna, Sweet Harriet and me. But not Madeleine. My baby was still in the clear except for this nervous breakdown. So we took her to Mexico and—"

"You've left something out." Seth's words snapped across the room and lashed at Flora's ears.

"I haven't left nothing out!" boomed Flora.

"Madeleine?" said Seth. "Hasn't she left something out?"

"Yes," said Madeleine, "she left something out." She turned to Peter and Robert.

"When they took me to Mexico, my darlings, I was five months pregnant."

"Mother," whispered Peter.

"Mother," echoed Robert.

Madeleine flung her arms out. "My boys! Come to your mother's arms!"

15

THE PUBLIC STENOGRAPHER slumped to the floor in a faint. Mallory and Loeb rushed to his side and propped him back up in his chair. As Madeleine hugged and kissed Peter and Robert, Loeb forced some brandy down the stenographer's throat. He came to, choking and struggling for air, then sighed and murmured, "Sorry. It was all too much for me."

"You said a mouthful, Buster!" snorted Flora. "Now settle down, boys. We're coming to the grand finale." She had no trouble winning their attention. "You can figure out what Madeleine's marriage to Sam down in Cuernavaca was all about. It was to give my grandsons a name. But like Fauna said before, we leaped before we looked. The boys were born a few weeks after Madeleine married Sam, just like it was with Fauna when I married Izzy. And too late we realized it wouldn't hold water with them Hollywood busybodies, trying to pass off the twins as Sam's kids. But Sam was here to stay as far as Sam was concerned. He wanted to be a director, and he was going to use Madeleine as a stepping-stone to that ambition. And if Madeleine tried to back away, he'd tell the world Barclay was Peter and Robert's father. You're named after your grandpa, boys, Bob Peters. When you were infants, I used to croon you to sleep with 'Roses of Picardy.' It used to put you both out in two minutes flat."

"Moulin Rouge," chuckled Pharoah.

"What was that?" asked Loeb.

"I said 'Moulin Rouge.' That's French for 'Red Mill.' 'Moulin.' Mill. Funneeee! Very funneeeee!"

With an impeccable air of hauteur, Robert sniffed in Pharoah's direction. "We had figured that one out for ourselves years ago, Mr. Love. But of course we couldn't be sure of our origins on that slender conjecture, could we?"

"No, cat. No court of law would buy it."

"But the 'Matilda Myelnitsa' ploy," said Peter to Madeleine, "was an enchanting inspiration. Myelnitsa, Russian for 'mill.' Moulin, French for 'mill.' Ah. The mills of the gods grind. How did you know the Russian for 'mill'?"

"Well," said Madeleine, "I once met Feodor Chaliapin—"

Mallory hovered over Flora. "Let's get to tonight."

Flora nodded and snapped her fingers at Peter and Robert. "Cigarette for your grandmother, boys."

Cigarette lit and smoke drifting lazily toward the strangely silent Seth, Flora resumed her narrative.

The police stenographer prayed he wouldn't be hit below the belt with any new surprises.

Loeb thought briefly and with great pleasure of the possible citations he and his two confreres might receive for having broken the case so rapidly.

"Once Madeleine hit it big again," Flora was saying, "she tried to push Sam as a director, and her studio gave him a chance with some quickie. It was rotten. Sam had always been a heavy drinker, but now it was getting worse. That and the gambling—"

"And the women," contributed Madeleine.

"Yeah, and the women. And Madeleine was paying the bills. Supporting Sam. Supporting Sweet Harriet. And by now Zelma Wave—because Barclay may have been dead, but he refused to stay buried. Every time a new murder broke out in Hollywood, they'd rake up Barclay's ashes. Sam was too smart to kill the golden goose now, and likewise Sweet Harriet. She couldn't get a job anywhere, and the hundred bucks a week she got steady from Madeleine—"

"Plus Christmas bonuses," Madeleine reminded Flora.

"Hell, yeah. Anyway, Sweet Harriet kept her sweet effing mouth shut. Still dreaming of the big comeback. Just like Fauna and me did, didn't we, baby?"

"We'll never make that movie now," sighed Fauna. "How sad."

"And that brings us to the present. Here's Madeleine in New York for a TV series, her first offer after that rotten Mozzarella business five years ago." Flora looked at Loeb and Mallory. "That dago hood on the West Coast. Her big chance to get back into the big time—and Sweet Harriet follows her here to put the squeeze on her to get her a big part in the series. And then Sweet Harriet starts working on Sam. He should be directing her! Then Madeleine gets *him*"—pointing at Seth—"to work on her memoirs. And then *they*"—pointing at Peter and Robert —"hit town looking for Barclay's murderer—"

"And our identities," Robert reminded her.

"O.K., O.K.," snorted Flora, "so now you're properly labeled. Does this make better men of you?" They later agreed Flora's statement was something worth contemplating. "Well, anyway, flatfeet, Sweet Harriet and Sam start putting the pressure on my baby, and I start worrying she'll go to pieces again. And she sort of started to. She tells Sweet Harriet she ain't never gonna play her kid sister in the series, and she tells Sam he ain't never gonna direct and that's *that*. Sweet Harriet meets with Sam this morning and then phones me she and Sam are gonna blow the lid off the Barclay Mill case and I see our world beginning to crumple. So Fauna reads the cards."

"They never lie," whispered Fauna, focusing on Seth. The smile on Seth's face was enigmatic and alien to Pharoah, and Pharoah wanted to be alone with him in the apartment and talk with him and reason with him and convince him of how great their need was for each other. But why this sinking feeling that talk and reason might no longer reach Seth?

"There was death in the cards."

"And the skull in the teacup for good measure," added Fauna.

"So I phoned Sweet Harriet."

"I don't believe you. You're lying."

"Listen to me, Sweet Harriet. This is right out of the horse's mouth. Madeleine's gonna make the announcement tonight at the concert and bring you up on the stage with her. You're gonna play her kid sister. She wants us to bring you to the concert and lead you up to the stage when she gives us the high sign. And let me tell you, kid, this comes right from the heart. Fauna and me are happy for you. We been thinking it over and talking it over and you deserve this break. You've been through hell, kid, and you deserve this break."

Sweet Harriet was weeping softly and Flora had the phone propped between her shoulder and cheek as she carefully knotted the rope in her hands, an inexpensive acquisition from the cut-rate hardware store on West Seventy-second street.

"Now, stop crying, Harriet. You want to look your best tonight."

"I'm going to call Madeleine," sobbed Sweet Harriet, "and beg her to forgive me."

"No! No!" shouted Flora. "She's sleeping! She had a rough night. Now, you meet us at that Good Humor wagon at that entrance to the park. And, Harriet . . ."

"What, kiddo? Dearest sweet Flora kiddo? What? What?"

"Not a word to anyone, you hear? Not even to Sam. We don't want to spoil the effect when Madeleine makes the announcement. It wouldn't be a bad idea if you took yourself a nap now. You want to look real sweet tonight."

"Oh, I will! I will! And bless you! And bless Fauna! And bless Madeleine!"

She hung up and did the thirty-second-time step. "I've won, Barclay! I've won! I'm coming back, Barclay! I'm coming back!"

"Miss Dimple? Miss Dimple?" The desk clerk was banging on the door. "You'll have to stop that screaming in there. Do you hear me? You'll have to stop that screaming."

"Then Fauna and me took the crosstown bus to the East Side and went to visit Sam. He didn't answer the door at first and we got a little worried, didn't we, baby?"

Fauna nodded. "Yes. There wasn't all that much time."

"But God was on our side. We heard Sam stumbling around, and he answered the door, stoned out of his head. Well—" Flora shrugged—"there was nothing to it. I socked him in the jaw and he passed out." Madeleine shuddered and Robert put his arms around her. "Then I broke his neck, carried him into the bedroom, and laid him at the foot of the ladder. His hand was kind of clenched funny like, but I sort of liked the effect, so I left it that way. Then I put his other hand around one of the rungs to make it look like he was trying to hold on to something. Not bad, eh, flatfoot?" she winked at Loeb. "Then we came back to our apartment, shoved the rope in the knitting bag, and— Hey, you." Pharoah's eyes drifted from Seth to Flora. "What was the giveaway in my knitting bag?"

"Fibers from the rope sticking to the wool."

"Well," sighed Flora, "you can't win 'em all. So right on the dot, there's Sweet Harriet at the Good Humor wagon. I bought one for Fauna and we headed into the park. Fauna and I had cased the place on our way back from Sam's, and we told Sweet Harriet that's where Madeleine wanted us to stay hidden till she gave us the signal. Well, it was a cinch. I started choking her, and she began struggling. Then her neck snapped, and we strung her up to make it look like a suicide. That part was a cinch. She was as light as a feather. Then, if you'll pardon the expression," guffawing heartily, "we tippy-toed away and went looking for seats. The concert had already begun and we didn't want to miss any of it."

"I saw them leaving the path." Madeleine shifted from Robert's arms to Peter's. "They didn't see me and I couldn't cry out to them. My voice was paralyzed. Somehow . . . somehow I knew what I'd find, and . . . and . . ." She drew away from Peter, fingers pressing against her throbbing temples. "Robert!"

"Yes, Mother?"

"Mother!" sighed Madeleine. "Oh, how I've yearned to hear that word pass your lips!"

("Sorry, Madeleine. We'll have to take that one again. There's a boom shadow on your face. Watch that boom up there!")

"Robert . . . Robert, it's not too late to phone Louis Nizer, is it?"

The phone rang and Madeleine jumped.

"Mallory here." He listened. "It's O.K., Sanders. We got the killers. You heard me. We're bringing them in now. No, I ain't got no needle in my arm. I got the confession. The works. No, Sanders. Wyndham's death was *not* accidental."

"Shit!" boomed Flora. "We might have got away with it!"

Madeleine sat quietly in her cell waiting for the twins to arrange bail.

". . . Accessory after the fact . . . act of concealment . . . hindering the prosecution . . . The D.A. in L.A. is asking for extradition. . . ."

Her head buzzed and she tried to find the switch that would clear the channel.

What happens now, she wondered. Flora and Fauna will go on trial in New York for the murders of Sweet Harriet and Sam Wyndham. Unless of course the District Attorney in Los Angeles fights to have Flora extradited to face trial in California for Barclay's murder. And I'm an accessory. I don't like that word. "Accessory" means gloves and earrings and handkerchiefs and diamond clips.

This cell means nothing. No one will understand that. No one. But I'm free, by Christ, I'm free at last

The matron looked in briefly at the sad little figure huddled forlornly on one corner of the cot, shook her head and continued on her rounds. Fauna drew the coarse blanket around her shoulders and re-examined the cards she had so carefully spread on the mattress. The jack of clubs had come up next to the ten of clubs and that meant she'd be receiving a surprise. Maybe I'll wake up in the morning and it'll all turn out to be a bad dream, like the "Through the Looking Glass" number in the *Follies of 1930.* Her brandy-drenched brain had ceased its torture half an hour ago, thanks to the Alka-Seltzer the matron had kindly supplied, but what about those other tortures for which there are no known remedies? What will I say to Sam and Sweet Harriet and Barclay when we come face to face again? We never did have all that much in common, come to think of it.

Bellevue.

Such a lovely name. It's like being in a beautiful mansion in Louisiana surrounded by magnolias and wisteria, and soon I'll hear the banjos strumming and Barclay will shout, "Roll 'em!" and it'll be my cue to sing "Bayou Lover, You're Swamping Me with Love."

She studied the eight of clubs. That meant money. "We can still turn a profit on this one, baby." Isn't that what Flora said in that nice limousine with the bars on the windows? We can sell our confessions to the newspapers and the magazines, and then maybe Flora will realize her dream of posing on a white bearskin rug for *Playboy*.

She yawned and wondered if she ought to try and get some sleep. I have to face those men in the morning. They're the ones who'll decide if I'm fit to stand trial. I wouldn't mind that at all. It'll be exciting and suspenseful and then maybe, like Flora said, we'll be box office again, baby. I like Flora's idea. I really do. Even Madeleine liked it. That big sign outside the courtroom: NO ONE SEATED DURING LAST FIFTEEN MINUTES OF TRIAL.

Flora turned over abruptly, hit her head against the wall and cursed. Damn cot's too narrow. She sat up, reached for her cigarettes and lit one. Maybe if we hadn't killed Sam. Sweet Harriet had to go, but Sam—who knows? On the other hand, once he heard about Sweet Harriet getting it, he might have gotten frightened and run to the police. The hell with it. No use crying over spilt milk. I hope my babies are all right. Madeleine's used to cells. But Fauna. She doesn't have her nerve pills. I'll have to get some new clothes for the trial. God, what a drab, dingy dungeon this is. I'll have to get the twins to go over to Alexander's and buy me some curtains. Where did Fauna dig up the nut act all of a sudden?

She sat up trembling.

Could my baby really be off her rocker? Did I drive her

to it? Is Madeleine sick, too? Where'd I go wrong? I only wanted the best for my kids.

Christ! Ain't they heard of Mother Love?

Get undressed, cat, and go to bed. That's the dawn coming up like thunder over there in Jersey. In fact, that's thunder. Why doesn't baby cat come home? He knows I won't sleep till he comes home.

("Where were you? Who were you with? Why'd you come home so late?")

I promise, Seth cat. No more questions. No more suspicions. You *do* have a right to your own life. You do. You do.

But where are you? You're off with them twin cats someplace, aren't you, cat? Why were you so quiet back there in Madeleine cat's hotel? You just sat there and watched when Flora cat had me pinned to the floor. She might have killed me, Seth cat. Didn't that occur to you? She might have killed me. She has a grip like a steel vise.

Is that it, Seth cat? Is that what you were hoping, sitting in that windowseat with that little cat smile? Where are you, you mother-fucking murdering son of a bitch! I could turn you in right now, don't you know that? Who gives a damn what they do to *me!* What the hell am I without you?

Come home, you son of a bitch, come home.

"Peter."

"Yes, Robert."

"I believe Mr. Piro has passed out."

"Seth," groaned Seth. "Call me Seth. It's so Biblical." He sat up and smiled at the twins. "I was, as I have frequently written and rewritten, lost in thought. What are you thinking, Robert?"

"I'm thinking of that lamp burning in the window of your apartment. I see Mr. Love pacing up and back frantically, wondering if he dare alert the Bureau of Missing Persons to your absence. He doesn't like us, does he?"

"What Mr. Love likes or does not like or cares or does not care is no longer important to me." He yawned and stretched. "Gentlemen, I thank you for your hospitality, but it's time I went home and put Plan A into operation."

"Peter."

"Yes, Robert?"

"I have a suspicion Mr. Piro is standing at the crossroads of his life."

Seth reached for his Scotch, drained the glass, smacked his lips and then formed an O with his thumb and index finger.

"On the button, Robert cat." He was standing and struggling into his jacket. "I'm free, by Christ, I'm free."

Peter's eyebrows shot up. "You're quoting Mother."

"And Mother knows best. I'm going home, I'm packing a bag, I shall take a taxi to the nearest precinct, and there I shall unburden what is left of my desiccated soul. Are you impressed?"

"Overwhelmed," said Robert. "And what about Mr. Love?"

Seth turned in the doorway. "As Joan Blondell said to Glenda Farrell in *Traveling Saleslady*, 'Every man for himself.' Good luck, boys. Look after the family."

He winked and left.

"We've a busy day tomorrow, Peter. Try and get some rest."

"I'll try. What in heaven's name are you writing at this hour?"

Peter looked over his brother's shoulder.

"Unique twins, male, early thirties, interested in meeting equally unique twins, female. Object, matrimony."

"Now, let me see . . ." murmured Uncle-Mommy, carefully studying the stills spread out on the kitchen table. Lad, A Dog stood in the doorway in his Japanese kimono, hair tousled and eyes still heavy with sleep.

"You've been up all night. What are you *doing?*"

"Figuring out the next two," said Uncle-Mommy matter-of-factly.

"*What* next two?"

"They always die in threes, don't they? Sweet Harriet

Dimple's dead—now there's got to be two more. They always die in threes."

Lad, A Dog studied the familiar movie-star faces spread out in front of his uncle. "What about Sam Wyndham? Doesn't *he* count?"

"He does *not*. He was *nothing*. Now, let me see. Which of these darlings has the death look about them? Heh heh heh heh," he cackled with relish, rubbing his palms together, "they always die in threes."

Zelma Wave seemed oblivious to the test pattern on the television screen. Francis K. entered from his bedroom, yawning and rubbing his pudgy cheeks, to investigate the whistling noise that had awakened him.

"Weally!" he exclaimed. This was followed by two tsks as he crossed to the set and shut it off. "Sitting up all night like this, Mummy! Faw shame!"

Zelma's head was slumped on her chest. Her hands rested in her lap. Carefully, so as not to awaken her, Francis K. wheeled her to her bedroom.

He pulled back the blanket and fluffed up the pillows on her bed and then turned to his mother with a warm smile on his face.

"Awise, my love, awise! Time for beddy-bye."

He shook her gently. "Mummy?" He knelt. "Mummy?" He felt her cheek.

His shrieks were heard in the apartment above and the apartments on either side. Two neighbors came running to investigate, and the third hid under her bed.

Francis K. sat on the floor at his mother's feet and wailed and wept and cried, "Mummy! Mummy!" over and over again, and the neighbors banged on the door shouting, "What's wrong? What's wrong? Francis K.! What's wrong?"

Francis K. knew what was wrong but didn't want to hear himself say it, because that would be the reality, and Francis K. had not been brought up that way.

So instead, in a quivering little soprano as he held a gnarled, ice-cold hand, he softly sang, "I saw you dive into Swan Lake, and sink beneath the turquoise blue . . ."

The too-jolly voice on the radio in the bathroom announced the time and the weather as Pharoah ran the tub. It was a sleepless night and a breakfastless morning, and he had to be at the Women's House of Detention in an hour. I'll break your neck, cat, he muttered to himself, I'll break your miserable neck. He opened a jar, sniffed the bath salts, shrugged, and poured a generous dose into the tub.

The radio and the torrent from the tap drowned out Seth's entrance. Pharoah didn't hear him enter the bedroom and remove an overnight bag from the top shelf of the closet. He didn't hear drawers opening and shutting or the sprightly tune Seth was humming under his breath.

In fact, as he was about to step into the tub he was startled to see the bathroom door swing open and see Seth enter with a cheery "Good morning." He didn't reply, because he was too startled watching Seth open the medicine cabinet and systematically divest one shelf of his razor, his shaving cream, his toothpaste and brush.

"You can have the rest," smiled Seth as he headed back to the bedroom.

Pharoah lunged, grabbed his shoulder, spun him around, and the articles spilled on the floor. "What the hell do you think you're doing?" Pharoah shouted. "Where the hell have you been all night? What were you doing? Who were you with?"

Seth pulled free. "None of your fucking business." He knelt to retrieve the articles. "To quote a very gallant lady and a never-to-be-forgotten star, 'I'm free, by Christ, I'm free!'"

He was too quick for Pharoah. He saw the bare foot heading for his face, caught it, and twisted the ankle. Pharoah howled in pain and his left fist came down like a trip hammer on Seth's head. Seth reeled back and Pharoah's right hand connected with Seth's cheek, the sound of the stinging blow muted by the blaring radio and the pouring water. Seth clawed at Pharoah's chest, making tiny ribbons of blood, and Pharoah yelled in pain as he struggled to grip Seth's wrists.

"Let go!" Seth shouted. "Let go! I know what I must do and you can't stop me!"

"You are going nowhere, cat. You are staying right here with me. You are *mine*. Everything that's me is all tied up in you. Stop struggling, cat, and listen to me. Listen to me, dammit! We can work it out. Whatever's eating you, we can work it out."

Seth brought his shoe down on Pharoah's bare foot and the pain rushed to Pharoah's brain and inflamed it with indignant, maniacal anger. He struck Seth in the mouth, then the chin, then spun him around, clutching his tie in a choking grip, with his free hand cruelly slapping first one cheek and then the other.

"I don't feel it!" Seth shouted through the pain and his tears, "I don't feel it, Pharoah cat! There's nothing any more—nothing!" His right hand flew to Pharoah's face, clawing at his cheek, his left hand found Pharoah's eyes, and a finger jabbed and found the target and Pharoah cried out in agony, hands flailing out and striking Seth in the chest. Seth reeled backward, heel catching in the bathmat. He felt himself falling backward, into the tub. His right hand caught something and he held on to it for dear life for a moment, then fell with a tremendous splash into the bathtub, pulling the blaring radio down into the water with him.

His mouth opened, but not a sound emerged. His fingers clawed the air as his body stiffened with the deadly charge of electricity conducted from radio through water to Seth.

Water slopped over onto the bathroom floor, and Pharoah's hand slowly dropped from the injured eye and covered his mouth and stifled the scream that tried to escape from his throat.

He couldn't remember later how long he stood there sobbing. He was able to recall finally leaving the bathroom and making a phone call and saying something about an accident and pouring a Scotch and lighting a cigarette and sitting naked by the window and hearing the echo of a familiar voice shouting, "I'm free, by Christ, I'm free!"

There were television cameras and newsreel cameras and reporters and newspaper photographers, and somebody swore those two smartly dressed women peppering the air with shrewd questions were Dorothy Manners and Arlene Francis. It was a beautiful autumn day and Flora, Fauna and Madeleine stood with three policewomen at the top of the stone staircase leading to the courthouse and smiled bravely for the cameras, while Peter and Robert surveyed with astonishment the crowd surrounding them.

"Mother looks unusually lovely, doesn't she, Peter?"

"Yes, Robert. It was kind of the District Attorney to delay mother's extradition to Los Angeles until after Grandmother and Auntie's trials. Poor Auntie. Had she been less enchanting with those psychiatrists, she'd have been spared all this hullabaloo."

"Nonsense, Peter. Look at her face. She's loving every moment of this."

Fauna's face was indeed aglow as she held Flora's hand. Flora's mind was on her Cassini original and she hoped it wasn't too frivolous for a first day in court.

"Get them inside," the attorney pleaded with the policewomen. "It's turning into a three-ring circus."

"Give them another minute," said Madeleine out of the side of her mouth. "It's our first appearance together in thirty-three years."

She squeezed Fauna's hand and Fauna suddenly threw her head back and laughed. She was fourteen years old again and Barclay was shouting, "Let's make this a good one, kids! Lets outfinale every finale we've ever done together!"

"Let's!" cried Fauna. "Let's make it the best finale ever!"

The scene was to be run and rerun on television and to become a collector's item among movie buffs. The crowd cheered and many wept and Peter and Robert silently agreed with the man behind them who said, "Will you look at them broads! They don't make them like that any more."

Flora, Fauna and Madeleine stood with arms interlocked, bellowing with zest, fervor and sincerity as they high-kicked with teen-age grace:

> *"Let's stick to-geth-er!*
> *To-geth-er we don't fall apart!*
> *Let's show the good old U.S.A.*
> We've got heart! *Heaaaaaart!*
> *HEAAAAAARRRRTTTTT!"*

GEORGE BAXT
His Life and Hard Times

On a Monday afternoon, June 11, 1923, George Baxt was born on a kitchen table in Brooklyn.

He was nine when his first published work appeared in the Brooklyn *Times-Union.* He received between two and five dollars for each little story or poem the paper used.

His first play was produced when he was eighteen. It lasted one night.

Mr. Baxt has been a propagandist for Voice of America, a press agent, and an actors' agent. He has written extensively for stage, screen, and television. During stays in England in the fifties and sixties, he wrote a number of films *(Circus of Horrors, Horror Hotel, Burn Witch, Burn)* which are now staples of late night television.

His first novel, A QUEER KIND OF DEATH, was published in 1966. His other novels include SWING LOW, SWEET HARRIET; A PARADE OF COCKEYED CREATURES; TOPSY AND EVIL; "I!" SAID THE DEMON; PROCESS OF ELIMINATION; THE DOROTHY PARKER MURDER CASE; and most recently THE ALFRED HITCHCOCK MURDER CASE.

Mr. Baxt lives in New York, is a bachelor, and is devoted to his VCR.

THE LIBRARY OF CRIME CLASSICS®

THE BEST IN MYSTERY— PAST AND PRESENT

BACKLIST

BEAST IN VIEW
BEYOND THIS POINT
ARE MONSTERS
THE CANNIBAL HEART
THE FIEND
FIRE WILL FREEZE
HOW LIKE AN ANGEL
THE LISTENING WALLS
A STRANGER IN MY GRAVE
ROSE'S LAST SUMMER
WALL OF EYES

William F. Nolan
SPACE FOR HIRE
LOOK OUT FOR SPACE

Ellery Queen
THE TRAGEDY OF X
THE TRAGEDY OF Y
THE TRAGEDY OF Z

Clayton Rawson
DEATH FROM A TOP HAT
THE HEADLESS LADY
THE FOOTPRINTS ON
THE CEILING

S.S. Rafferty
CORK OF THE COLONIES
DIE LAUGHING

John Sherwood
A SHOT IN THE ARM

Hake Talbot
RIM OF THE PIT

Darwin L. Teilhet
THE TALKING SPARROW
MURDERS

WRITE FOR FREE CATALOG

Available at fine bookstores everywhere.

Unless otherwise noted, all books
are rack-size paperbacks, and $4.95.
To order by mail, send the list price plus
$1.00 for the first book and 50¢ for
each additional book to cover postage
and handling to:

INTERNATIONAL POLYGONICS, LTD.
540 Barnum Avenue
Building 2, Floor 4
Bridgeport, CT 06608